THE BINKLE AND THE CATAWAMPUS COMPASS

FAITH LYNELLA

books that zing

An imprint of Off the Page Press

COPYRIGHT

The Binkle and the Catawampus Compass
Faith Lynella (1944)
Also published as Dr. Lynella Grant and Lynella Faith Grant

Book 1 of The Binkle and Magic series

Print Version ISBN-13: 978-1888739633
ISBN-10 1888739630

Electronic Version ISBN-13: 978-1888739602

Publisher: Off the Page Press
Waltzing Words is an imprint of Off the Page Press

Websites http://faithlynella.com
http://offthepagpress.com
http://seizethesparkshirts.com

DEDICATION

TO EVERY LIBRARIAN
who ever encouraged a child
to fall in love with reading

TO THE POWER OF THE BINKLE
May binkle power brighten the lives and
deeds of everyone who knows about it

TO YOU, THE READER
I hereby bestow a bucket of binkles
upon you and all you love

CONTENTS

ALLUSIONS* ARE NOT ILLUSIONS

Some of Jeep's earliest memories are of his mother reading to him. Those were warm and happy times. Sharing stories together helped him develop his imagination and sense of adventure. Is that true for you also?

Books remain Jeep's favorite pastime. Since he reads so much, he notices if events in his life resemble scenes or characters from his favorite stories.

SPOT THE ALLUSIONS

In the book, Jeep makes allusions to books and characters he's read about. Did you spot some of them? Finding allusions is like an Easter egg hunt. Your mind is looking for connections between things all the time. How does this and that relate? What's similar? What's different?

Noticing such associations reveals much more than just what's right in front of our eyes. Start looking for those connections. They're there. And finding them is a binkle.

Allusions mean a particular term refers to something different. For example, saying "a person's nose is growing" could imply Pinocchio or lying. To say "the sky is falling" could refer to Chicken Little or seeing everything as scary.

CHAPTER 1
OVER THE EDGE

WHAM!
CRASH!
SMASH!

The earsplitting sounds echoed through the woods. They are followed by the tinny scraping of loose rocks that hit anything in their path, in their chaotic push to the bottom.

"Uggg… Aaagggggggg…" Cries of pain are accompanied by more crashing and scraping noises… The clattering racket is punctuated by the splintering of more branches. All of which is followed by rocks and tree limbs tumbling to the ground below.

THUD! OOMP! "Urrrrrrgg…" It is accompanied by indistinct crashing, branches breaking. and pebbles scraping. The racket bounces back from all directions.

SLAM! Then total silence—except for the pebbles that continue to rain down on the fallen body.

The terrible incident happened quickly. In no more than half a minute it is over. (Though the flattened tumbler probably felt as though the fall was going on forever.) Not that you can ask him— he is dead to the world.

Rolling the scene backwards: one moment the soon-to-be-battered person is balanced much too precariously on the unstable edge of a steep cliff. The next moment, he loses his teetering balance. His efforts to snatch a branch that could save him only hastens the inevitable. Then the ill-fated fellow's inert body bumps against everything in his way, as it plummets to the earth below.

It slams into every rock or tree big enough to have broken the fall. None of them did. Somewhere on his tumble, he was knocked out cold.

Somewhat later, that unfortunate person wakes up in a thorny thicket in the dark of night. His first thought is *"Owwwww!"* That is his second and third thoughts, as well. In fact, that very thought isn't far from his mind for days.

His banged-up body hurts in places he never had reason to notice before. And his spinning head is in no condition to sort out much of anything. He is pitiful—pure and simple.

The battered body belongs to Jeep. And his head-over-heels fall was courtesy of his dog, MeToo. Him and the darned truffles.

Every day after school (where he attends the sixth grade), Jeep "works" in the large park not far from where he lives. His job is to grow truffles—a fancy type of mushroom.

To this day, no one in the world understands how to cultivate truffles successfully. But Jeep's stepfather, Chris, expects to get rich from figuring out how it can be done. Chris has been chasing that dream for years—long before he married Jeep's mother.

To make Jeep's job harder, he must carry out his "farming" in secret—like in a spy movie. Nobody who comes to the park gives Jeep a second look—just the way he wants it. The boy looks ordinary in every way—from his short, curly brown hair, to his downcast eyes, to his ability to fade unnoticed into the background. Nothing about him stands out, making him as good as invisible.

Chris repeatedly warned him to be careful about being found out: "Secrecy is essential! If anyone finds out we're actually growing truffles… Well, let's just say lots of greedy people will stop at nothing to find out what we know."

Jeep can only look after his truffle patches when the coast is clear. Playing with MeToo provides a good cover. At other times, he leans against a tree, reading some adventure book he always carries along with him. People in the park assume he is just fooling around—but in truth he is tending to his chores.

At the start of their farming activities, Jeep couldn't figure out why Chris made so much fuss over truffles. They sure didn't look like much. The blackish, knobby, mushroom-like fungus grows wild on the roots of oak trees. Specially trained pigs or dogs sniff them out under the ground, so their keepers can carefully dig up the valuable truffles before they can gobble
them up.

Chris explained that the truffles' musky smell drives people mad with romantic desire. Gourmet chefs can't get enough of them for their la-de-da cooking. And since they aren't raised like other crops, truffles are rare and ridiculously expensive (even hundreds of dollars a pound!).

Their "farm" is spread all around the park, wherever the full-grown oaks grow. It's mostly hidden in out-of-the-way spots. Nobody else has a clue what they're up to. Jeep relies on his compass and his hand-drawn maps to keep track of their underground patches. Many of them had been in place for years—with not much to show for it. So far, anyway.

Chris and Jeep often labored late at night in the corner of the basement they grandly called "the laboratory." Using an old microscope and simple lab tests, they compare countless combinations of soil, fertilizer, and spores (tiny truffle seeds no bigger than dust), as they try to figure out which works the best.

It's up to Jeep to keep precise records of all the growth data they collect. So, he regularly checks the patches for signs of growth. As with most scientific discoveries, lots of tedious work must happen before discovering just the right "lucky" combination.

Whenever Jeep grumbles about doing so much boring work, Chris says, "We're getting nearer all the time. We've got to be close to success, we've just got to…"

Still, Jeep wonders, *if we're so close why aren't we seeing more truffles?* But he is smart enough to keep such doubts to himself. Between school, his truffle duties, homework, and so many chores around the house, Jeep hardly finds a moment when he can read what he wants.

Yet the drearier his life, the more Jeep counts on adventure stories to transport him to distant places and happier times— where heroes triumphed and magic was real.

It is already late afternoon when his dog approaches him with what appears to be a large truffle in his mouth.

"Hmmm... Where'd you find that, MeToo?" As Jeep reaches for what he is clutching in his jaws, the dog pulls way.

"Hey! Give!" The dog scampers away, leaving Jeep no choice but to follow.

MeToo never looks back or slows down until he reaches a cluster of trees shrouded in shadows. The dog stops suddenly at the edge of a steep drop-off. Jeep finds himself in a gloomy and overgrown place that is totally unfamiliar. A clump of tangled oak roots dangles over the edge.

I don't remember this place, and I was sure I knew every bit of the park by heart. Jeep pulls out his ever-handy compass, trying to figure out their location. No dice, he can't get an accurate reading.

"OK, MeToo, let's have it." Jeep bends down and pats MeToo as he reaches for the truffle. The dog backs away—to the very edge of the overhang.

Jeep smiles his annoyed-but-patient smile, while reaching for the truffle yet again. His voice is quiet and slow, to calm the excited dog.

"C'mon. Good dog! Where'd you find that?"

Expecting to get a hug along with the praise, MeToo eagerly springs against Jeep's outstretched right hand. The jolt knocks the compass out of his left hand. Jeep can hear it clatter down the steep incline, gathering speed as it goes.

As he looks over the edge, Jeep can't tell where it landed in the hazy shadows. *No way I'm leaving that here. Gotta climb down. There's probably still enough light...*

Jeep speaks to MeToo, as sternly as he knows how. "Sit! Wait here! You hear?" The dog isn't known for obedience—quite the opposite.

MeToo sits. But his tail end wags around so steadily, it can't be described as sitting still. Jeep turns his back to the dog, hoping the sternness of his voice can restrain MeToo's urge to follow.

"Stay MeToo! Don't follow me," he repeats as he looks back.

With his first footstep down, Jeep can tell the descent will be slow going. Between the cliff's steepness and the deepening shadows, he can't see even one step ahead. He must place each foot with care, and he can feel the unstable dirt shifting underfoot.

More than once, loose rocks slide ahead of him and descend into the gloom. Then several rocks from higher up hit him.

"Oh no," Jeep groans, as he glances up quickly enough to see MeToo's front paws anchored just at the edge of the cliff. The dog's wide eyes are fixed on his master.

"Stop! Don't move!"

The disobedient (and seemingly deaf) dog keeps thrusting his legs forward, sending down more pebbles. A clump of dirt dislodges, slides forward, and ruins Jeep's shaky balance. MeToo's large, unblinking eyes are the last thing Jeep sees before he plunges downward.

Consciousness drifts in and out in wisps, after his ungraceful tumble. Horrible images of his own splintered bones and torn flesh flood Jeep's mind. *At least I'm alive; that's something.*

But then he grimaces, whether through pain or sadness. *Not that anybody would care…*

Once Jeep can bear to find out how bad off he is, he mentally checks himself over. Joint-by-joint, limb-by-limb: *left hand— OK; right hand—OK; left arm—OK; right arm—OK; left leg…*

"Owwwww!" His leg throbs below the knee, where sharp branches had ripped his pants.

Could have been worse, I guess. Mostly bumps and scratches—except for my leg. But, how can I get back up that hill on it? The cliff seems to grow steeper the more he worries about his not being able to climb it.

I've gotta get myself out of this mess. But nothing's gonna happen 'til morning. And I'm too tired to care right now.
So, he dozes off again.

As he swims in and out of consciousness, Jeep can't ignore the rumbling in his stomach. It isn't the first time he's been hungry. But then, hunger isn't something a person ever gets used to. What bothers him more than starving was feeling so helpless and alone.

For the zillionth time, he wishes for his mother and resists the urge to cry. *Cold as it is, my eyes would probably freeze. And why make myself feel worse than I do already?*

Every time Jeep wakes up in the cold darkness his mind leaps from one dismal thought to another—the only part of him capable of leaping. *I sure feel rotten all over... Chris is going to kill me... I'm just a lost, unwanted orphan...*

That isn't exactly true, but it is close enough. His gloomy thoughts wanted to revisit that horrible night the year before when his life unraveled. By sheer determination, he manages to avoid going there.

Instead, fuzzy thoughts swim in and out of his muddled awareness. During conscious moments, all sorts of worries

14

marched back and forth in his mind—*I'm in trouble now...
Where am I?... Is MeToo OK?...*

Thoughts of MeToo bring the dog's helter-skelter image to
mind—knee-high, with brown fur and large white patches,

a stubby tail that wags nonstop, and big ears that flopped.
From the first day they got him, MeToo followed Jeep
everywhere. So, he named himself.

Jeep can't help but smile, thinking about how his dog greets
him—with a joyous, bouncy dance on his hind legs and
tongue hanging out.

Thinking about MeToo just makes Jeep worry more—for
both of them. *He's out there lost and hungry, just like me. If (I
mean when) I get out of here...* But he can't think clearly for
long or figure out a plan that could work.

The chill wind blows through Jeep's clothes, making him
burrow deeper into the drifted leaves for the slight
protection they provide. *It's cold as Narnia out here,* he frets.

Jeep tosses and turns, unable to find an even slightly
comfortable position. He crawls around in the dark, feeling
for a flat place with fewer brambles. His stiff fingers bump
against his compass, which he already assumed was gone for
good. The familiar way it fits into his hand reminds him yet
again of his mother.

He could recall getting that compass several Christmases
past, just as clearly as though it happened yesterday. It

wasn't the largest box in his pile under the tree, but it had the fanciest paper and ribbon.

Even before he opened the golden wrapping, he hefted the package in his hand and felt it belonged there. He remembers opening the gold layers of wrapping so carefully that the paper didn't tear.

As he held his compass for the first time his mother told him, "You're never lost when you've got a compass along."

Guess that means I'm really not lost. No way to use this tonight, but it might be handy come morning.

That is his first comforting thought of that long, long unpleasant night.

CHAPTER 2
IT WAS A COLD
AND WINDY NIGHT

At some point during that chilly, miserable night, Jeep remembers what some hero he'd read about did in a really tough fix. *Why the heck not try it? This sure looks like a tough fix to me.*

Jeep scrunches his eyes tight—hoping against hope for something magical to happen. Then he wishes himself out of this horrible mess and safely home—wanting it more than anything else in the world.

As slowly as he possibly can, he takes three deliberately slow, deep breaths—in… out…, in… out…, in… out….

Jeep waits at least a minute without moving a muscle before timidly opening his eyes. Nothing had changed. *Nothing! I'm still lost, still hungry, and still in the dark.*

He ached more with disappointment than from his body's aches. *What a fool! But I was so sure something had changed. I was so sure…* But the evidence all around him can't be ignored—everything is just as before.

A combination of anger and foolishness washes over him. *What did I expect, anyway? Magic? Who do I think I am? Harry Potter? That kind of stuff only happens in fairy tales.*

Until then he hadn't quite admitted how much he has counted on a magical escape. Now even that fanciful hope is gone. Yet another crushing disappointment for a boy afraid to expect anything else.

Uncomfortable sleep fades in and out. Sometime later, Jeep is awakened by rustling sounds nearby. *Probably an animal... more scared of me than I am of it.* In his fogginess, he thinks he feels a bump against his sore leg more than once. *More than likely, it's my imagination is working overtime.*

As the first daylight filters down through the dense treetops Jeep looks around for the first time. He can't believe what he sees. It isn't natural—that's for sure. A broad mass of wild creatures crowded around him and extends well into the shadows. None of them move.

Ohmygosh! I didn't imagine all these animals. They're everywhere! I suppose I'd rather have critters near me than be here by myself. But what do they want?

Time passes slowly and it never really gets light—just a fuzzy grayness. Jeep tries to sort them out—skunks, raccoons, squirrels, birds, rabbits, and a few furry lumps he can't quite identify.

His heart jumps as he sees the light reflecting from what has to be more than a hundred shiny eyes. *They're all staring at me!* He wants to ask them, *What are you doing here? What do you want from me?*

The leaves covering him slip aside as he awkwardly sits up. Jeep stretches his stiff arms out and swings them around to get the blood moving. Then he blows on his hands and slaps them together.

It helps a bit with the coldness, but does nothing for his hunger. His wiggling around makes the animals back away, but not much.

As Jeep fidgets about he feels a slight stirring against his hip. A mouse had crept into his pocket. Jeep's left hand slides down and fondles its fuzzy warmth.

"You can stay," he whispers. "At least one of us is cozy." Jeep likes the idea of protecting a furry friend. He doesn't feel so helpless as he rolls the tiny mouse in his palm and marvels at its warm softness.

Suddenly, the silence is broken when all the animals chatter, mew, chirp, and yip at once. Their cries grow louder until they blend into a steady, pulsing drone.

Then, as quickly as the hullabaloo started, it stops. Complete silence! With a single movement, all the animal heads turn in the same direction.

Jeep looks where they are looking too. "Huh?!" He rubs his eyes and looked again. *That can't be real! I must be dreaming… or it's from this dim light.*

There seems to be a shimmer coming toward him. As it gets nearer, Jeep sees the oldest-looking man he ever saw. He stands no taller than a child, but in every other way he seems ancient.

At least a zillion wrinkles crease his face, which is softened by a waist-long beard and bushy white eyebrows. The man's dark green hat flops to the side, and his shapeless coat is at least a hundred years out of style.

But what made the man impossible isn't his weird appearance, bizarre as it is. The man does not look solid. He shimmers. One moment he looks normal (well, normal is a stretch, but at least he looks heavy enough to stand on the ground). The next, the light is passing right through his body.

But that's not the strangest part. The man trips and falls apart—into shattered chunks.

Jeep hears him say, "Kittens hendrini!"

The next moment, the man seems to be back together, just like nothing happened. So, Jeep assumes his eyes must be playing tricks on him. What else could it be?

The approaching figure bounces along, barely touching the ground, like a balloon lifted by a breeze. The wooden staff he carries towers over him—obviously he doesn't need it for walking. *He's strange, no question about it. The way he moves is even weirder.*

The stranger (a strange stranger, perhaps) isn't alone. A brown and black dog, resembling an oversized Doberman, walks on his left. As the dog came closer Jeep notices something is fastened on its back. *A saddle?* And an ordinary-looking brown rabbit hops along behind.

When the trio is almost up to him, the man seems to trip again. The sound of "Kittens hendrini!" is the only indication that Jeep isn't having an eye problem.

With the little man so close, Jeep watches the whole weird chain of events as if it is happening in slow motion. What looks like tripping is more like a cracking apart, as if the man is no longer in one piece. His wrinkled face contorts in pain, like he's being stung by hundreds of bees.

When he says the kitten thing again SNAP! He comes back together again. It probably only took a second—but it seems to be much longer. *If this is real, I've got no clue how the world works.*

The procession stops when it reaches the circle of animals. The wrinkled man pauses and looks kindly over the assembled critters. When he spreads his arms wide, his open mouth lets loose a garble of deep rumbling sounds. But it seemed to lack words. Even so, what appears to be a speech rises and falls in a steady rhythm, "Ooobo dobooo roonoo besoooboo alooooocoooooo…"

Jeep thinks it sounds more like wind as it blows through the trees than any human language. But while he can't follow the message, the assembled animals seem to. Their rapt attention is fixed on the wrinkled man as though they understand every syllable.

His arms gesture as if he's making a speech or performing some ceremony. The man chants in that way for several minutes before he falls silent. After he slowly nods toward the crowd, he waves goodbye in a wide, noble gesture.

With that signal, all the animals hop, crawl, fly, tiptoe, and slink off—fading silently into the underbrush.

Only after the last animal vanishes does the stranger turn his attention to the boy. Jeep isn't sure whether he should be scared or not. *Am I in danger or about to be rescued?*

The strange man is in no hurry to make up his mind. He thoughtfully rubs his beard while he studied the still-reclining figure from top to bottom—and then back up again. The scrutiny doesn't stop at the skin, either. Jeep could feel the man's eyes look right into him, almost like X-rays.

Now what? He's sure taking a long time—but I'm afraid to speak first. Jeep looks the old man over as well. But he isn't the least bit clear about what to make of what he sees.

Eventually, although the long-drawn-out silence isn't broken, Jeep senses that the man has reached some decision.

"Hungry, Laddie?"

Jeep nods. *At least he speaks English. I was starting to wonder.*
The man's poking around in the many pockets of his
shapeless coat reminds Jeep of circus clowns who pull
countless objects from their bottomless pockets. Finally, the
wrinkled face breaks into a satisfied smile as he dramatically
brings out what he's spent so much effort hunting for—a
single cookie.

"Harrumph. Here—eat this." The man's rumbling voice
seems much too large and deep for his miniature size.

"Thanks, Mister." Jeep doesn't hesitate, despite a half-
remembered warning against taking food from strangers.

Jeep pinches off a crumb of the cookie before he shoves the
whole thing into his mouth. *Not bad, but not nearly enough.* He
secretly slides the crumb into his pocket so the mouse can
gobble it from his fingers.

"Where am I? How'd ya find me?"

"Harrumph… Follow me, Laddie" is the only answer he gets.

Jeep feels powerless to resist the man's commanding voice.

Besides, he badly wants to trust him. *Maybe he can help me get
home.* As Jeep starts to rise from his lumpy bed of leaves he
stumbles, loses his balance, and falls back down. Both legs are
asleep. His knotted-up muscles all scream *No!… Leave us
alone! It hurts too much!*

His next try Jeep grits his teeth and stretches forward with extra care. The stranger pokes his extra-tall staff at the struggling boy. Jeep ducks away before he realizes that it isn't being done to smack him. Then he grabs the staff to steady himself. After several false starts and clumsy maneuvers, a wobbly Jeep finally stands.

"Can you walk, Laddie?"

"Sure. I think so," Jeep insists with more confidence than he feels.

With that, the man and his animals turn back in the direction they came from. Jeep slowly limps behind them, leaning on the staff.

A warning voice pipes up in Jeep's head, *Should you trust this guy? He's awful weird. But then, everything's weird tonight—the fall, his arrival, and all those animals.*

Although he can't think of a single good reason to trust the wrinkled stranger, Jeep ignores his grumbling doubts and stumbles onward.

The odd little man dodges around rocks and trees as though following a trail that is invisible to Jeep. Sometimes he vanishes, only to reappear further ahead. Jeep strains to stay close, but it is tough going on his tender leg. He finds it easier to watch the dog since at least it stays solid.

The strangeness kept repeating itself. The occasional sound of "Kittens hendrini!" reminds Jeep that this weird person didn't belong in the world he's used to. And that isn't the only clue.

Jeep whispers to the hitchhiking mouse. "Sit tight. I'll get us out of here—somehow. Just don't let him see you." His brave, protective words make Jeep feel a tad bolder.

Although they don't cover all that much distance, Jeep's leg hurts so much it seems like a very long way to him. Jeep can't tell what direction they are going since everything in the dim, overgrown woods looks the same to him. There is no way he'd be able to retrace his steps.

At one point, the little man steps behind a large boulder. But when Jeep reaches it, he freezes. There is no one there! And the path has ended.

He disappeared—gone! Even though there's no place to go! I'm lost again!

All the fears the boy managed to thrust aside during his dark hours of suffering rush in. Jeep sinks to his knees— exhausted, discouraged, and weary to the bone. *No more! I can't stand any more, I just can't!*

At the point of Jeep giving up, the stranger's voice calls out "This way." His wrinkled face pops out of a hole which has been hidden in the rock's shadow, not far from Jeep's feet.

The sight of the head without a body startles Jeep, making him titter with nervous relief. When the bodiless head vanishes again Jeep hurries to follow.

Climbing down into the underground crevice is rather tricky, making his tender leg hurt even worse. *Gosh! Seems kinda like falling down a rabbit hole.*

Jeep finds himself in a rock tunnel, which isn't dark for some reason. Once out of the biting wind, Jeep feels much warmer. He pats the mouse in his pocket and whispers, "See, not so chilly down here. Wanna bet we'll run into a white rabbit?"

The rock ceiling (which is plenty high for the man) is so low Jeep has to walk bent way over. Since the staff is so tall, he drags it along behind. Most of the way, the tunnel is so narrow he can run his fingers along both rock walls at the same time.

In the confined tunnel, the puzzling phrase, "Kittens hendrini!" echoes back to Jeep several more times. The reminder of the impossible cracking apart (then uncracking), on top of his fright and exhaustion, is just too absurd. Jeep fights the urge to giggle insanely. *I've clearly lost my mind.*

As Jeep limps along in an awkward crouch, an idea arises that both scares and excites him at the same time. *Maybe I'm having an adventure! Maybe it's magic! I've certainly wished that it could be real often enough.*

Any free moment he could find, Jeep had his nose in a book. His favorites were daring adventures from olden days that involved heroes or magic—better yet, both. He believed such fantastic things could happen, even to him. So, somewhere deep inside him, a mixture of hope and longing stirs—just a little, but it stirs, nonetheless.

Though he struggles to walk bent over, Jeep no longer fears he'll get lost. He just needs to take the next step—taking all the time he requires.

After a while the tunnel levels off. Jeep hears the strange stranger say, "I almost didn't get back in time." But he can't hear the muffled reply.

So, he knows they've arrived. But where?

CHAPTER 3
LIFE BENEATH THE OAK TREES

The strange stranger holds aside a heavy woven tapestry, while he gestures impatiently for the boy to enter. Jeep pauses, as a wave of apprehension washes over him. Hope wars with fear.

What lies behind the curtain for me? Danger or rescue? Is it a trap I won't ever get out of?

Hope won out—giving him just enough courage to step over the threshold. That and his body's yearning. *At least I'll be getting warm again—and maybe fed.*

Jeep found himself in a cavern high enough for him to finally stand up straight. He can't see anything except the fire in a fireplace. He also hears and smells the crackling of wood that's burning in it. Jeep recognizes other smells as well— kind of cinnamony with a hint of fresh flowers.

There's enough dim light for him to tell the room is carved into solid rock. Yet tapestries and a patchwork of rugs manage to add a warm, homey feeling that "softens" the rock. Together with the heavy wooden furniture and cabinets standing against the walls, the whole room could best be described as old and comfy.

Before Jeep has a chance to sort out more details, the man grabs his arm and drags him to a table overflowing with books and papers. His host uses one arm to shove aside the stacks, and with the other he thrusts the bewildered boy onto a rather low padded bench. Jeep wonders for the hundredth time, *what have I gotten myself into?*

"What…?"

"Eat first, then we'll talk."

Another hand (though all Jeep saw was a yellow blur) sets a full bowl of something and a spoon in front of him. *I don't care what it is. I'll eat anything that doesn't bite back.*

Jeep takes a mouthful but doesn't recognize the taste. "What is this?"

"What would you like it to be?" the old man replies.

"Chocolate pudding is my favorite."

"Then eat chocolate pudding."

And that's exactly what the next bite tastes like—creamy, chocolaty, and just sweet enough. Jeep eats until he can hold no more—though it took three full bowls. The strange little man sat across the table from him and idly strokes his beard.

He never takes his eye off Jeep, as he watches the food disappear. Not a word is said, and his face gives no clue that betrays what he might be thinking.

As soon as Jeep finishes eating, the man leaps to his feet and drags the boy away from the table. The unexpected jerk brings Jeep's fears back full force.

When they come to a corner of the living area, the little man says, "Clean yourself, Laddie. You'll feel better."

Behind a curtain, there's a basin filled with warm water and a primitive potty. Once he is alone, Jeep lets his mouse friend eat the gob of pudding he has hidden in his hand. The lapping of its little tongue sort of tickles.

"Sit tight. I'll protect you," Jeep whispers. How he could manage such a feat, if necessary, is wishful thinking. But just saying the words gives Jeep's confidence a small boost.

By the time Jeep washes up, his curiosity is working overtime. *Where in the world am I? And what does this guy want with me? I've got a lot of questions....*

As Jeep limps toward the fire he gets his first glimpse of a woman sitting near the old man on the sofa facing the fireplace. The two of them have left a place for him in the middle.

The woman looks even older than the stranger, as if that were possible. Her face's web of interwoven wrinkles reflects a very long life span, filled with challenges. She is knitting from a large ball of soft blue yarn. Seeing the needles flashing with the reflected light from the fire reminds Jeep of his mom. She knitted, too—used to, anyway.

The woman's light-colored hair is braided, then looped round and round her head so many times it resembles a turban. She has a way of looking old and young at the same time. She, like her male companion, seemed to shimmer in the flickering firelight.

Except for being tiny, as far as Jeep can tell everything about her seemed normal enough. *Though I'm not sure what normal is anymore—certainly not tonight.*

"This must all seem strange to you," she said, as if reading his mind. Her voice seems as high and breathless as the chirping of a bird, "Don't worry, you're safe here. So is your mouse friend. Go ahead and let him run around. The cats won't bother him."

How did she know? Jeep reached into his pocket and set the wiggling mouse on the floor. Once free of the protective pocket, the mouse scampers off and took no further notice of him.

The old woman's dark dress looks as if wildflowers are embroidered all over it. With masses of blooms, it is the most colorful place in the room. Jeep is sure that he smells flowers.

Puzzled, he leans forward and sniffs several times.

She notices his curious sniffing and laughs. "You like flowers, do you? So do I. Sweet peas and bachelor buttons would suit you." The woman plucks several fresh, living blossoms off her skirt and hands them to him. Jeep inhales their fragile perfume while he strokes the delicate blossoms with the tip of his index finger. *As far I can tell, they look and smell like real ones.*

"They're as real as I am," she said. *Uh-ho, does that mean that neither of them is real? Or both are? It's confusing—so hard to be sure.*

The little man interrupts his pondering as he hands Jeep a mug of steaming hot chocolate. The first sip is hot enough to push away the recollection of being nearly frozen to death. But the taste... *Wonderfuller!* (a phrase from mom) *I never tasted something with my whole body before. It tastes good even to my toes.* Jeep lost himself in the delight of sipping.

"Harrumph... Welcome, Laddie. My name is Grikkl. Here is my wife, Adah. We're gnomes." His voice is so deep it rumbles, as though it echoed back from even deeper in the earth.

Jeep tensely clutches his cup with both hands as he sips his cocoa.

"What should we be calling you?" Adah asks.

"Jeep Parker," he answered timidly. "Actually, it's Jasper, after my grandfather. Jasper Elliot Parker. J-E-P. But everybody calls me Jeep."

"Tell us about yourself."

Jeep is too tongue-tied to answer. But if he had answered, it would have included some of these facts.

> Jasper Elliot Parker (Jeep)—11 years, three months old; weight, 91 pounds; height, four feet, ten inches; blue eyes; curly brown hair. Attends sixth grade at Lincoln

Elementary School, in Truman City, Ohio. Earns above - average grades, and biology is his best subject. He is an only child whose father died four years ago. Lives with his stepfather (Chris Thompson) since his mother (Helen Thompson) is hospitalized. Has been an eager reader since he was seven. Hasn't exhibited any obvious talents, although he likes to sing. His favorite possession is the marble collection inherited from his grandfather (who he's named after). Can touch his tongue to the tip of his nose. Doesn't play on any athletic teams, but is a reasonably good sport.

That sums up the bare facts of Jeep's life. But it didn't describe the way the gnomes saw him.

He has endured great sadness for one so young. Still believes in the power of wishes and magic. Can move with the grace and speed of a leopard. Is good at solving complicated riddles. Is starved for kindness and attention. Loves to daydream, especially about flying and heroic deeds. Doesn't trust himself, and lets his fears blind him to everything else. Has yet to learn how he is special. Is already blessed with powerful abilities that he hasn't yet discovered.

The two gnomes read the boy's simple heart. So, they can feel what was good, and healthy, and hopeful about the lonely child who sits between them. The gnomes had the wisdom to trust the twist of fate that brought them together. But that doesn't mean they could not also recognize the heart-breaking difficulties ahead for Jeep as well.

"I've got some questions...," Jeep starts to say.

"I'm sure you do—plenty of time for that later," Adah replies as she gently pats his hand.

"I've got to get home, it's really late."

"All in good time, child, all in good time."

"But I'm in trouble. I can't stay here."

"Not yet. You have time for more hot chocolate and a song."

Almost out of thin air, another cup of the steaming exquisiteness appears for him. How could he refuse? Not possible since every cell of his body tingles with the delight of it.

"Relax for now and listen. I learned this melody from the mermaids long ago, when they taught me how to hear the music of the sea."

Adah's eyes grew dreamy and far away as she remembered back. "There aren't many mermaids left, you know."

The sounds coming from her lips resembled the movement of water more than a human voice. The surging and receding waves swished like the ocean currents. At first Jeep thought he couldn't follow the words, but gradually he felt it weave its images into his mind, without words at all.

The splashing water sounds conjures up images of wind and surf, and frothy foam. He recognizes the quieter sounds within the swishing water of fish swimming, each one leaving a bubbly trail through the flowing water. And he can hear the crash of waves against the rocks, a ship's engines passing overhead, and the calls of the ever-present gulls. The longer he listens, more and more oceanic sensations flooded his mind.

Even though he had visited the coast several times before, Jeep knows he is really "hearing" the sea for the first time. Not hearing as much as sensing. Sensing with every speck of his flesh and awareness involved. Even the water in his cells and blood recognize the sea as part of himself.

By the time Adah completes the song, Jeep is totally relaxed. And so, with almost no words spoken between them, Jeep sinks into a deep peacefulness.

"I see you're ready to sleep," Adah says. She arranges a cot for him near the warm fireplace. Then she tucks him in and gently smooths his hair.

The thoroughly exhausted boy doesn't sleep soundly. Instead, he sank again into the nightmare that had become his life. He relived the horrible night it started.

A long scream jolts Jeep awake. *What's wrong?* Another spine-chilling scream proves he isn't dreaming. Both his feet hit the cold floor even before his eyes open. In the bedroom next to his, Jeep's pajama-clad mother flails about on the bed. She shrieks again.

Jeep sees Chris, his stepfather, leaning across her as he slaps at her wrists again and again. *What did he do? Why would he hurt her?*

"Mom, you OK?" Her eyes are open but she doesn't seem to hear him.

"Listen to me! You've got to listen!" Chris yells with a brutish intensity loud enough to be heard above the shrieks. She pays no attention to him, either.

"What are you doing to her? Can't you see she's in pain?" "Jeep, I can't make her stop! Call 911," Chris groans.

After he makes the call for an ambulance, Jeep asks "What now?"

"I wish I knew… Nothing works." Chris's face is ashen— etched with fear.

More screams and thrashing about by Jeep's mother only deepen their uncertainty about what more to do for her. Not many minutes pass before Jeep opens the front door to insistent banging. Three uniformed medics brush past him, as he points toward the bedroom.

Jeep watches one of them insert a needle into his mother's arm. Her hysterical screaming stops. The desired silence brings Jeep no comfort, however.

Going through their well-practiced routines, the team efficiently lifts her onto a wheeled cot and roll her limp body out to the waiting ambulance. Its flashing red and white light makes Jeep's head spin, as he slips further into an eerie, unfamiliar world. One marked by fear and helplessness—one where time seems to stand still.

After Chris and the medics climb in and close all the doors, the ambulance slowly pulls into the empty street. Barefoot and still in his pajamas, Jeep stands at the curb under the glaring streetlight. He watches helplessly until the red-and-white flashing lights disappear into the darkness.

Jeep wrestles with his fears the rest of the night. Sleep is unthinkable. He doesn't feel like going to school when the time came, so he decides not to go. There's not much an eleven-year-old can do to help at such a time, but Jeep feels the need to stand by—just in case.

For breakfast that morning, Jeep makes pancakes for himself, just like his mom used to make them. With colorful candy sprinkles she called "crumbled rainbows." He even heats the syrup like she did. Although he isn't all that hungry he wants to pretend she is there making his breakfast—like always.

Jeep sits at the table eating his pancakes. But midway through he starts to sob and can't get another bite down.

He can't stop thinking about his mother or her weird ways of doing absolutely everything. She bragged about being *unpredictable on purpose* because she was steadfastly anti-habit.

She'd say, "If you aren't careful about them, your habits will take over your whole life. And that's what shuts your brain off. Look at all the zombies walking around with distracted eyes. That's not being alive—their habits took them over."

Helen would explain that as long as a person does a task differently every time (not the easiest or fastest way, mind you) the "habit gods" can't get in control of his or her life. So, she was constantly inventing silly and strange ways to sweep the floor, or make a bed, or wash her hair. Like rinse before you wash, or stand on one leg the whole time.

Jeep loves that about her. He misses that quirkiness about what she would do, as much as her ever-cheerful, can-do attitude. Every day used to be full of surprises that way, instead of the dull and tedious way they became without her.

An exhausted Chris drags himself home from the hospital about noon.

"Mom OK?"

"They can't tell yet. They have to do some tests. She's sleeping now—that's all I know."

"But when do I get to see her? When is she coming home?" Chris just shrugs and shakes his head. A sorrow rises up in Jeep that is both sharp and unbearable—a feeling which has since taken up residence in his heart. Mom is gone, and there isn't anything either of them could do about it.

No matter how often Jeep asked about his mother in the days that followed, Chris never tells him anything specific. From those non-answers, Jeep suspects that her illness has to be serious—too terrible to put in words. The dread of it gives him the shudders whenever she comes to mind.

Gradually, by silent agreement, Chris and Jeep stop mentioning her at all—even to remember back to the time before....

Since that awful night, a whole year has passed—without Jeep hearing from her even once! Unbidden thoughts of her just bring back sadness for him, while stirring up fears that lurk just out of sight.

Instead, he'd daydream about how things were going to be when... So, little by little since then, Jeep pulls back into his private, lonely world, and only speaks when he has to.

Day time? Night time? It's impossible to tell which. Being underground without windows, Jeep quickly lost his sense of time. Upon awakening, he has no idea how long he's been asleep. But the first thing he notices upon emerging from drowsiness is the brown rabbit that's curled upon his chest. Its long ears are pressed against his ribs.

Adah sees Jeep stirring. "That rabbit adopted you, Jeep. See that? What her ears are doing? She's listening to your heart."

"What's her name?" His fingers drift through the rabbit's downy fur, as he rubs her neck and ears.

"Since she's claimed you, it's for you to name her. Give her a name in your language, anyway. She'll answer to it. I've no idea what other rabbits call her."

Jeep thinks a moment. "I've always liked Lulu."

He lets the word roll around his tongue. "Lulu... Lulu..." Then pleased with the sound and sense of it, he lifts the rabbit so their noses touch.

"You're my Lulu." In reply, she holds his gaze without shifting a hair of the hare—like they are shaking hands on the deal.

Grikkl introduces Jeep to the dog that came along on his rescue. It stood taller than Grikkl himself, and was obviously bred for speed.

"We call him Cerberus after the mythological dog that guards the gates of the Underworld[1]. He's gentler than he looks— unless you have wickedness in mind. In that case, watch out."

Cerberus stretches his head forward and rubs it against Jeep's hand, making it easy for his fingers to scratch it. Rubbing the dog's ears reminds Jeep of his own dog and the sadness of being lost. *Finding MeToo is the first thing to do when I get home.*

---

[1] Cerberus – pronounced sur´ ber us, the guardian of the underworld from Greek mythology; a monster with three heads (sometimes said to have 50 or 100 heads), a snake for a tail, and a serpentine mane

Almost like a mind reader, Adah leans over and whispers in Jeep's ear, "Don't worry yourself about your own wee dog. He's safe—you'll see."

"Really? That's great," he replied with relief—without thinking to ask how she could know that.

"Relax. There's no need to rush. There's plenty of time for you," she said. "There's an unusual time-space state down here. Trust me about the details, but believe me when I say the folks back home won't be worrying about where you are."

"That would be nice, though hard to believe. But there's nothing I can do about it now," Jeep conceded.

"Well then, don't give it another thought."

The household also included a raven named Ramses, who perches above the fireplace and looks majestically down upon everyone. Adah's two black cats are called Heather and Yawn.

As far as Jeep can tell, they are always asleep side by side. Both being black, it's impossible to tell where one cat ends and the other starts. So, Jeep thinks of them as a single big lump of cat.

Later, when Jeep tried to remember back to his time at Grikkl's, he could never recall the cats having moved from exactly the same spot. The cats are alive, no question about that. But they're as active as the furniture.

A while later, Grikkl brings Jeep more food without being asked. The boy takes a spoonful and rolled it around his mouth without recognizing the flavor.

"What is it?"

"What would you like it to be?"

"Chicken noodle soup sounds good."

"Then chicken soup it is."

It's exactly the way Jeep likes it—with chunks of white meat, wide noodles, with lots of chopped celery. But there's an unfamiliar taste too.

This stuff might taste like things I love to eat, but this isn't ordinary food. Not by a long shot!

Later, Adah tells Jeep a bit more about herself and Grikkl. "Grikkl's nearly 800 years old; and I'm even older. We never had any baby gnomes. Wanted them, but it never happened. We came to America during the 1700s. Imagine making a new start in life when you're already 500 years old! Once in a while, we return to Europe and visit Fairyland, our true home."

But what they'd done before then or since then was left rather vague. Jeep could hear longing in their voices whenever the couple would speak of the olden times and distant places.

Although they both answer Jeep's questions, their replies leave him with more puzzles than he started with. He got the impression they were holding something back from him.

But Jeep is holding something back as well, since he hardly ever says a word about himself or his life at home.

Over the next days, Jeep falls into the gnomes' routines. But he isn't entirely convinced that he won't be in trouble once he gets home.

Mostly Jeep eats and rests while his strength returns. Adah gives him small tasks to help her, like sorting moonberries or grinding up smelly herbs he can't begin to guess the uses for. Her busy hands never slow down as she tells Jeep strange and wonderful tales.

Jeep fidgets and mumbles whenever Adah inquiries about his life at home. Since she can tell he isn't ready to talk yet, she's waiting until the time is right.

They both seem content for her to do most of the talking. And Grikkl? He hardly says anything at all, as he works away on his piles of books and papers.

Twice a day, Adah rubs a purpley, gloppy, strange-smelling cream on Jeep's sore places. Wherever she touches him, he can sense little tingly energy bursts that pulse beneath his skin.

Feels like my cells are jumping up and down with pleasure. They love what she's doing— and so do I.

Adah proudly confides, "I make the cream myself. Trust it to 'cure whatever ails you.'"

"That cream probably works OK. But it doesn't get all the credit for fixing my bruises."

"Oh? Really? What does?" she asks in puzzlement.

"Your magic. It's there, isn't it?" He softly touches her hands— almost in awe of the enchantment he senses in them.

"Aye, magic!" she answers with a wink. "But it could be the magic of caring."

"That too, no doubt. But you can't fool me."

She simply smiles back at him in a most enigmatic way.

Jeep asks Grikkl why he kept saying "Kittens hendrini!" on their walk to his home underground, but he hasn't heard him say it since.

Instead of answering, Grikkl acts embarrassed and shakes his head. After it comes up several times, Grikkl finally replies.

"Oh, you saw? I was afraid of that. Can't be helped, I guess."

"So, what was it?"

"Well, let's just say, there's something special about this place where Adah and I live. I don't have a problem as long as I stay nearby. But when I have to go into the human world, keeping myself together gets rather tricky.

"How so?"

"There are parallel universes, you know. Sometimes I get caught between them." Grikkl snaps his fingers. "That fast, I fall out of this one—barely hanging on."

"I thought I saw something happen. But you don't really come apart. Right?"

"It's hard to talk about. Almost feels like being in more than one place at once. I have to really concentrate so all of me stays together. One moment of forgetting—snap! I start slipping into different dimensions. After that I need a spell to put myself right."

"Sounds terrible!" *And impossible.* "But you're in the real world."

"Maybe… You'll come to see Laddie, that a lot depends on what you think 'real' is."

"Sure, that makes a lot of sense," Jeep says, but his expression indicates he really doesn't think so.

Adah brings out an old book with stories of a white knight named Laarik, and his trusty sidekick, Holger. The knight rides the countryside vanquishing evil and rescuing more than fair maidens. Old, young, hags, children, critters—Laarik is in the rescuing business in a big way.

Using his magic powers, he and Holger turn everyday objects into whatever is required to save the day. In most of the stories he shows that a person doesn't need strength as much as common sense to find a solution.

Whether Laarik confronts dragons or wicked villains, the knight finds a way to leave a trail of tranquility behind him. So, it all turns out OK.

It is Jeep's favorite kind of adventure, and every time he picks up the book it changes so it tells him a different tale than the last one.

"I can't believe I never read about Laarik before. This book wasn't in my school library."

"I'm not surprised," Adah replies, "the *Tales of Laarik* are quite popular in Fairyland. Since he's a gnome, you know."

"Oh... I didn't get that."

Morning and night do not mean much in a place cut off from daylight. The ordinary passage of time makes no difference so far underground. Sunrise and sunset passed without notice. Since the food tasted however Jeep wanted, meals gave no clue about whether it is breakfast time or dinnertime.

But each meal also brings a reminder that he really needs to get home. Chris is sure to be worried by now, and who knows what people would be doing to find him.

Eating continues as a high point for Jeep. Somehow, the texture of each dish matches whatever flavor he wants. But how could that be?

Adah explains that what he'd been eating provides plenty of healthy vitamins and minerals, no matter what it tastes like. He just has a choice about the taste of it.

All my favorite foods, one after another—pizza, brownies, chocolate sundaes, macaroni and cheese, whatever I want.

He figures out the more he likes something, the more flavor it has. So, if he wants a meal to taste like liver and onions (that he hates) it probably wouldn't have much flavor at all. But why waste a chance to have a favorite treat, just to test the theory out?

A large grandfather clock with six round dials on its face stands against the wall near his cot. Jeep can't figure it out since none of the dials resemble the clocks he knows. Some of the dials have no recognizable symbols. Others show pictures that change every so often—a flower, a bird, a bell, a hat.

Jeep asks Grikkl, "How does this clock tell time? It's too strange for me to figure out."

"Don't worry about that. Those dials provide information about Fairyland. And none of them measures time the way you're used to. Just forget about time while you're here."

"That's not hard to do. Since I came, I've pretty much forgotten about the rest of the world. And I don't want to go back to it, either."

In a light-hearted mood Grikkl confides, "Adah's not the only one who makes music."

From behind his back he pulls out an undersized, deformed accordion. As he pulls it in and out and strokes its buttons, unearthly sounds pour out. The instrument looks to be as old as Grikkl. In two shakes, the underground living chamber echoes with an old Celtic tune, as he plays at a frenzied pace. Grikkl's fingers move so quickly they seem to blur together.

Jeep cannot keep his foot from tapping in time. Even though he's never danced before, he cannot sit still. He and Adah whirl around the chamber together. By the time he's played a string of peppy tunes, a winded and tuckered-out Grikkl needs to rest.

Once he catches his breath, Grikkl says, "I don't play often enough, even though it feels so good when I do! This fine concertina deserves to be heard. Her name is Arla. She has her own mind, you know. Plays what she pleases, sometimes melodies I don't even know."

He holds the instrument out to Jeep. "Touch that. Feels like wood, doesn't it?"

Jeep slides his finger over the surface. "Feels like wood. Certainly not plastic. So, what is it?"

"What you felt with your finger is the woven essence of thousands of songs. It's music made solid. Not just songs—but the merriment of the singers, the joy of the dance. All that resides in Arla.

"She was a gift from King Bedwald, after I rescued his daughter from the trolls. That was way, way back, when I was still a young gnome. Whenever I play Arla, I feel every bit that young again."

CHAPTER 4
TIME STANDS STILL
FOR A WHILE

Jeep offers to help clean up, but Adah shakes her head.

"The way I run the house is pretty easy. There's not much cleaning involved. The enchanted logs burning in the fireplace provide our light and heat. There's nothing for me to do about that. Those oil lamps go on or off at a snap of my fingers."

Adah doesn't cook in the fireplace—or anywhere else. "The special food you like so much is called "faduki." It looks like a bag of ready-to-eat sawdust when it comes from Fairyland.

"All I do is add enough water to make it stick together in whatever texture I want. Making pudding or soup uses a lot more water than bread does.

"For something like cookies, I just pat the damp faduki into any size or shape. As you figured out, I don't need to worry about spices, since everybody tastes the flavors they like. But sometimes I serve nuts or vegetables for a change."

Water to the cavern comes from an underground spring high above them. Adah only has to decide how hot she wants the water to be in the rock basin.

Dirty dishes (or clothes, for that matter) would march themselves through hot, sudsy water, climb onto the drain, then spin around until dry (they seemed to like that part). Then they march back to where they belong.

Adah shows Jeep a cabinet where she puts the garbage. Whatever is placed inside crumbles to fine dust that blows back out to the upper world through a chimney of some sort. She calls it nature's kind of recycling—with nothing wasted.

Though he can't see them, Jeep knows there have to be air vents somewhere, since the air is always as fresh and pure as anyone would expect in an enchanted wood.

Like someone sharing a closely guarded secret, Adah whispers, "Here's how most of the work around here really gets done." She points at an intricately carved wooden basket on the mantle. Jeep can't quite see what what's inside, but he can tell it is yellow.

Adah croons, "Nelda, Nelda, Nelda, Nelda, Nelda…," like one calls a cat.

Jeep hears a droning hum. Suddenly, the "whatever" in the basket wiggles, followed by a flurry of darting movements. Soon, a finger sticks up from the basket—then another, and another… With a single graceful motion, Adah scoops up the wiggling "whatever" in both hands and rubs it against her cheek with gentle affection.

"Oh, Nelda, so glad you care to join us. This is Jeep." Nelda stops patting Adah's cheek long enough to wave a single finger in his direction. Friendly or warning, he can't tell.

"Jeep, meet our Nelda—she's a hand-over." He sees a loosely stuffed yellow glove-like shape about the size of a pie.

Adah places the whatever on the floor, instructing, "Put everything away, Nelda. Then dust and sweep, if you please."

Nelda buzzes louder than before, as it (or she?) sets to work. She whizzes around the room. Jeep can't take his eyes off the hard-working, nimble hand-over. Sometimes she made somersaults or high leaps to cover the distances quick as a wink. Jeep got the impression of her dancing on her fingers much of the time.

Adah beams with appreciation. "I'll bet you'd like a Nelda of your own, wouldn't you, Jeep? Sorry, but I couldn't imagine life without her."

"You're right. I want a Nelda, who wouldn't?"

"So, now you know why everyone in Fairyland (where Nelda's kind live) can spend so much time playing."

After supper, Adah and Grikkl sit Jeep down in front of the fireplace and gather around him. "It's time to tell you about the powerful energy Grikkl and I rely upon. Tonight, you'll learn about a remarkable force, a force that heals, a force that can resist evil. A force which has immense power—power to make remarkable things, wonderful things happen. You'll take your first step to learn a well-guarded secret."

Grikkl announces, "It's called…," and he mimics a trumpet sound, "da de da dum de da…" followed by a long pause. "The binkle!"

"Binkle? What's a binkle? I've never heard of it," says Jeep.

"Exactly so, Laddie. And that's a great tragedy. The binkle exists to bring joy and caring into people's lives—and yet its existence is almost unknown among humans. The binkle is the energy that's created whenever beings connect in a special way. Like with you and Lulu. You know, that moment when you feel a special closeness."

Adah adds, "The binkle is the energy that's created between you. You feel a little click inside when you sense a connection with another part of creation. It could be with a person, or a creature, or a tree, or a stone, or the great rolling sea. That feeling makes you want to smile with your whole self."

"What does it do?" Jeep asks again. "I don't get it."

"It's not about doing. It's more about feeling. That sense inside when you know things feel 'right,'" said Grikkl.

"I know you've felt binkles, Jeep—everyone has," Adah adds.

"A moment of joy, a moment when everything makes sense—then, you sense a tiny zizz of energy. Like an electric current deep inside. Binkles are tiny, very small and easy to miss. But get enough of them and things begin to change—inside you and around you. Pay attention to the energy you feel—whenever it happens. That's the first step."

"But isn't that just feeling happy?"

"You begin to see a bit. They're often found together."

"Happy energy. Like when you sing to me?"

"That's part of it, but there's lots more going on as well. You'll spot binkles whenever there's a zizz that makes you feel truly alive."

"Ohhh…K. You've made it all clear now," says Jeep, as he rolls his eyes and nods in a way that indicates exactly the opposite.

Meanwhile Back at Home…

Chris leaves work mid-afternoon without saying a word to anyone. He doesn't rush as he clears the papers off his desk. Then he slips out the side door without looking back.

Chris slides into his eight-year-old car and sits for several minutes, clenching and unclenching his hands on the padded steering wheel.

After he relaxes enough to face what awaits him, he drives north into the country. He is a man on a mission—a mission that brings him no joy.

Ten minutes later, Chris pulls off the main road into the grounds of a fortress-looking complex. After the guard at the gate waives him through, he parks and locks his car. Then looking neither left nor right, he climbs the stairs and enters the building.

Chris knows what he's come for. Yet his stiff movements and clenched jaw tell even a casual observer that he's forcing himself to go forward.

It is the third Wednesday of the month and he is visiting his wife (as he does every first and third Wednesday).

The nurse on duty greets him. "Oh, Mr. Thompson, your wife's doing fine today. Her hair's done differently, so you might want to comment on it." He just nods.

Chris enters an office with "Accounts" painted on the door. The clerk looks up as he drops quietly into the chair by her desk.

"How much this time?" she asks without any greeting.

"Two hundred-fifty dollars is the best I can do right now," as he hands her a check.

"You've fallen behind," she comments with disapproval. He fidgets in his chair, like a kid sent to the principal's office. All too true, but the best he can do.

"Maybe next month...," the very same words he had said to her the month before. She glares at him and gestures for him to leave.

Once out of the office, Chris marches with resolve through the echoing halls. He stops just outside his wife's room and pauses long enough to straighten his back and bend his lips into a smile. Then, like an actor who moves on stage, he opens the door and steps through.

"Hello Helen. I've missed you."

He walks over to her narrow bed. "Still in bed? No, that won't do. Here, let me help you into your chair."

With gentle tenderness, he lifts her from her bundle of blankets and places her in the padded chair by the window. He sticks a pillow against the side arms to keep her from slipping sideways.

"No roommate yet, I see. That's too bad," he says as his eyes fall on the vacant bed against the opposite wall. It's been a long time since anyone else shared her room. "I hate you being alone so much. You need company."

Chris arranges her chair to permit the best view out the window, even though it just overlooks parked cars. Only then does he bend over to kiss the top of her head, before sitting down on the metal folding chair nearby.

"Helen, it was a beautiful drive over…" he begins. "Jeep is doing fine in school—got an A on his biology report, about lizards, I think. It looks like he'll get his truffle survey done before the snow falls…"

Early on, Chris had hung up a little bulletin board of photographs that had special meaning for her. Today he adds a recent school picture of Jeep.

"Nice looking boy, don't you think, Helen? Your eyes, your smile."

Mentioning Jeep makes Chris feel guilty. He knew he wasn't much of a father to her son, even though he intends to be. Besides, Jeep is an uncomfortable reminder of the woman he loves, but who is so far out of reach anymore. Chris doesn't dislike the boy, but their relationship is strained without Helen around to make them feel like a family.

Chris had no experience being a dad—not that he had big shoes to fill. Jeep never knew his real father. Helen treated her first husband as a brief presence in her life, so had rarely mentioned him.

He tells her the latest about the truffle project—not sparing any of the details. "As soon as that money starts rolling in I'll get you out of here, Helen. We'll find the best specialist; they'll know what to do. And then we'll be a family again."

on this and that poured from Chris, more to fill the empty silence than anything else. He knew better than to stop talking, because then it would be obvious that the only words spoken are his.

He stands up and paces back and forth on the worn tiles, as he carries on his impersonation of a conversation.

A while back, Chris taped up a poster of a ferry boat above her bed, to act as a reminder of a perfect day. His eyes linger there now, as he recalls the first time he'd seen her—on the Bayside Ferry. She wore a fuzzy pink sweater over her slacks. Her flowered scarf kept flapping because she faced into the wind the whole time.

Chris and Helen were the only passengers who didn't duck into the warm ferry cabin. She stayed outside for the view— and he stayed outside because she did.

He traced all his happiness back to that unforgettable day. *Now it's all been pulled away from me and I have to act like I can stand it. I have to carry on as though anything matters—which it doesn't—not anymore.*

And although such thoughts keep coming to mind, he can't let on—not to anyone. Not even to himself.

Chris pulls his mind back to the present, into the gloomy room and a sadness he cannot ignore.

This woman is the right size and pretty enough—but she's not my Helen, who's been gone for too long. This person can't smile or talk to me. And there's no reason to think she hears a word I say.

Early on, the doctor told him, "Your wife might be alert sometimes, so don't do or say anything to upset her."

That's why he took care to put on a cheerful false face. But each visit left him with greater despair.

Just to be here with you reminds me of how much I've lost, how much it hurts inside.

 To him, she'd always be like her famous namesake—Helen of Troy, the face that launched a thousand ships. He used to tease her about that. But it never was her face that he found most appealing. He loved her lighthearted energy. Even strangers could feel it, without quite knowing why.

Chris's heart responded to that quality about her right away—lively, alert, filled with curiosity. Sure, he liked her, but he especially liked *how he felt about himself* whenever they were together.

I couldn't believe my good fortune when you liked me back, then loved me back, then married me. And to be honest, my life wasn't that great before then.

He recalled them eating a pizza about a month after the day on the ferry. *You smiled your sunny grin, our eyes met, and I knew— just knew "She's the One." And apparently, that was precisely when you knew, too. Your love's the bright spot of my life. Our three years together were the happiest I've known—that is, until you came here.*

Now… Don't go there, he reminds himself. *Don't even think about going there.* But he can't stop remembering back—to the good times.

Chris was fed up with the doctors—irritated, actually. He hated the unemotional way they spoke of Helen's illness or their predictions about her recovery ("not to be expected"). In the beginning, they implied they'd make her better—and then they didn't. *They're not trying hard enough; you're no better than when you came.*

The medical experts treating her used technical terms like "schizophrenia" that really didn't explain anything. Even though her illness came on quickly they implied there must have been signs—if anybody had been noticing.

Well—there hadn't been any. None at all! And until the awful night Helen broke down, neither of us saw it coming. I can't put much trust in doctors or their scientific mumbo-jumbo. They haven't fixed you, and it looks like they never will.

Although Chris started out every visit determined to stay cheerful, it was nearly impossible to keep it up. Before long his tortured feelings would bubble up and his self-control deserted him. He had to go right away. He kissed Helen goodbye before rushing away with tears glistening in his eyes. Visits to see her took all the stuffing out of him.

Sadly, Chris never told Jeep any of this. So, the man and the boy each suffered their cheerless grief alone.

CHAPTER 5
INSIDE THE CHAMBER
OF ANCIENT WISDOM

When Jeep could walk easily without pain, Grikkl asks him, "Ready for an adventure?"

"Sure, but aren't I having one already?"

Grikkl hands the boy one of his heavy woolen robes. The arms are long enough, but it is cut so short it fits Jeep rather like a jacket. *Wow! That's right. I'm a kid but already a lot bigger than Grikkl is.*

Once they get bundled up, Grikkl walks up to a cavern wall. With a flip of his wrist he pulls back a bright tapestry. Jeep sees a door cut into the otherwise unbroken rock—with nothing but a large keyhole on its rough-hewn surface.

Grikkl inserts the heavy key dangling from the golden chain around his neck. The door quietly swings open, away from them. Ahead Jeep can see nothing but darkness.

Cerberus leaps eagerly into the opening. Adah hands a lighted lantern to Jeep and another to Grikkl. After they stepped into the passageway she closes the wall behind them with a solid thunk.

They walk single file—first Cerberus, then Grikkl, then Jeep. The ceiling of the tunnel is high enough for Jeep to walk without having to squat down. The narrow tunnel twisted at odd angles, sometimes going up and sometimes going down—shifting direction for no apparent reason. Jeep stumbles over the uneven footing and twist his ankle more than once.

However, Grikkl doesn't have any difficulty, and bounces along, barely touching the ground. Jeep notices there isn't any of the kittens hindrini cracking up by Grikkl, either.

Cerberus impatiently leads the way, as he repeatedly runs ahead and returns to them, before running off again. Jeep's mood echoes the dog's high-spirited eagerness. *I can't wait to get there, even though I don't know where we're going.*

Although the tunnel is cut through solid rock, in some places the ceiling is shored up with heavy timbers. Tiny rivulets leak down the rocky walls here and there. Jeep dodges drips from overhead, and a few times he needs to leap across places where water is puddled.

Every so often, Jeep sees unfamiliar letters painted on the rock walls. *Could these be road signs for gnomes? I wonder what they say. Or maybe we'll run into a bunch of dwarfs down here.*

When Jeep asks what they say, Grikkl just grunts. Although Jeep never found out exactly what the symbols meant, he later would encounter similar figures all over the underground domain.

Before the procession has gone very far, the tunnel ends at a solid wall of rock. Cerberus sits down—with the patience one feels while waiting for the traffic light to change. Grikkl puts his lantern down, freeing his hands.

He majestically raises both arms upward, then chants, "Gaggoob boonaaa taamooloodem…" Grikkl repeats the melodious cadence four times. His voice is so deep and low it sounds almost like the earth itself is groaning.

At the end, Grikkl drops his arms and picks up the lantern. For a long minute, nothing happens. But then Jeep notices a tremble underfoot, followed by a rumble, then a breeze. Ever so slowly, the rock slides back just wide enough for the three of them to slip through.

Once on the other side of the rock wall Grikkl claps his hands in an irregular rhythm. The rock closes behind them, leaving no sign it ever moved.

Jeep was getting used to such unexpectednesses (so does that mean they cease to be a surprise?). *It's just the way magic works*, he reminds himself, no more amazed than he would be for the arrival of an elevator back home.

The procession continues its downward journey until halted by another wall of rock.

This time Grikkl blows musical notes (ta-ta-tee-ta-dum) on a whistle hanging next to the key. Like before, the rock wall creaks and moves aside. On the procession goes, down, down, down, ever deeper into the earth.

Why are so many protections necessary, I wonder? Surely no one could get in here if they're not supposed to. Jeep's thoughts are interrupted when they reach two massive wooden doors that block the passageway. Each door has its own keyhole and they look exactly the same.

At this obstacle, Cerberus takes charge. The dog sniffs around each door and makes tiny woofing sounds. He pauses to listen and would then bark more loudly. Cerberus repeated the process as he ran back and forth between the doors.

To Jeep's ears, the only sounds he could make out were the ones caused by the dog. Finally, Cerberus stretches out in front of the left door.

Grikkl pats Cerberus, "Good dog," as he inserts the key around his neck into the left-hand door.

Grikkl says to Jeep, "One of these doors is enchanted and leads to The Path of No Return. I've never figured out where it ends up, but there's no way back to this world from there. But it's not the same door every time.

"Even I don't know which one is safe on a particular day. But I can always trust Cerberus to make the right choice."

The heavily-carved wooden door swings forward, opening into a large rock chamber. Inside it's so black that their lanterns can't penetrate the darkness. After they enter and close the door Grikkl mumbles a moment and gestures with his hands. The candles on the walls begin to burn, making the room as bright as twilight.

Jeep and Grikkl snuff out their lanterns, leaving them by the door. Jeep asks, "Why do you bother with lanterns if you can just wag your fingers?"

There are spells in the tunnel."

Jeep rolls his eyes and says with exaggerated pleasantness, "Oh yes, that explains it." *Just another answer that doesn't explain anything.*

Grikkl marches around and through the mystifying piles of strange objects stacked everywhere in the large cavern. Jeep can barely contain his curiosity as he gawks around.

Most of the chamber is still in shadow, but Jeep can tell it is huge. The ceiling is probably 20 feet high. In the dimness, Jeep can't even see across to the other side.

As soon as Grikkl reaches an area arranged for sitting, he again works his lighting spell with quick hand motions. As he settles in, he signals for Jeep to do the same. By the time Grikkl gets his feet propped on a nearby crate, it's evident they won't be leaving for a while.

"Where are we, Grikkl? I feel like I said 'Open sesame!'"

"You're righter than you know, Laddie. Some of this stuff was in that cave as well. I've brought you to a place with priceless and irreplaceable treasures—every one of them remarkable in its own way. These objects are one of a kind and most of them influenced the course of history in a positive way.

"They're not mine, just so you know. I'm merely their caretaker, sworn to protect them." He sounds a bit in awe of the responsibility, as he gazes across the vast collection with respectful amazement.

"Wars. Battles. Quests. These things you see here were often present, sometimes as the prize. Or at least they were nearby as a witness to events that were changing the world of their day. Many of those stories have been faithfully retold in history texts and legends—no doubt with some exaggeration. Grand stuff..."

His attention wanders off to the ancient past. Jeep waits in respectful silence—although not patiently. Later, with a shake of his head, Grikkl pulls himself back into their present place and time.

"Before we can go on, there's something I need from you."

Grikkl straightens in his seat and assumes a solemn expression. "Promise me... Promise me, Jeep, you will never tell anyone that this place exists, or about what you see in here. Even to know about this chamber puts you in a very small group—most of them not human."

"You can trust me not to tell."

"Tskkk! What kind of vow is that?! It's a dead-serious oath I'm asking for. People have died defending this secret."

"I get it. I get it—my lips are sealed! I will not tell anyone about this place or what I see or hear in here. Ever."

"Certain?"

"You can trust me, Grikkl. Honest."

"I think you're right. That's why we're down here, Laddie. I am trusting you." Grikkl's face brightens and twinkles as he drops his stern manner.

"The official business is done. So, go have a look around. Just be careful—many objects are very old and fragile. Whatever you handle, put back exactly where it was."

Jeep doesn't need to be told twice. Poking through piles stirs up a billow of dust. He sneezes and reaches into his pocket for a tissue.

Instead, Jeep finds his compass and pulls it out without thinking. From long habit, he tries to get a fix on North. The compass needle keeps spinning around, never slowing down or stopping. Jeep shakes it several times but the needle won't act normally.

Grikkl is watching and laughs out loud. "That won't work down here, you know. There's no way you'll ever get an accurate reading."

"Because we're way underground?"

"No—it's the concentration of high-vibration energy here. That's what's making your compass go catawampus. Lots of other things can't work here either, like clocks and radios."

"Because it's magic...?" Jeep ventures. *Anything strong enough to mess with magnetic forces has got to be pretty powerful—or magical.*

"Something like that."

Jeep's attention is attracted to a pile of swords, shields, and helmets stacked as though ready for a tournament. He fingers a badly scratched shield, feeling the coldness of the coarse texture and the deep gouges along its surface.

Wow! These scrapes probably happened in battles where ordinary people fought—maybe even died.

He imagines himself as a daring knight in early England, as he struts about holding a round shield and swinging a short sword. When he puts on a helmet he cannot see hardly anything through the narrow slit before his eyes. Jeep can barely hold his head up because of its heavy weight, and the helmet's sharp bottom edge gouges into his shoulders.

So heavy! How could anyone move around in this and still fight? I'm sure I could've done it, though. I'd have liked being a knight.

Jeep yells, "Hey Grikkl, is some of this stuff from Camelot?"

"How could you tell?"

"Any chance you knew King Arthur?"

"No, a bit before my time. That was about the Sixth Century A.D, and I'm only 800. A really long time ago, that was."

"Hard to think of you as too young. Only 800. Good one!"

Some historians argue that King Arthur and Camelot never happened, that they were just a myth. But I never believed it. This stuff proves it! This is the solid, touchable history.

Nearby, Jeep finds heaped-up trunks and crates that overflow with pirate treasure—gold coins, jewels, elaborate carvings, and gold bars. And over there, stacks of framed pictures that show knights and warriors engaged in deeds of valor. And there, Indian relics… And over there, rugs and tents… And there, stack after stack of thick, aged books… And here, and there, and there…

Wherever his eye lands, Jeep sees one incredible wonder after another. A person could spend years and not see it all— let alone getting into all the crated-up stuff.

I can only guess what's in all those boxes and piles. Like I'm in a king's treasure house. No doubt, there's an amazing tale that goes with everything that's here.

Grikkl busies himself gathering some heavy books and rolled parchments. Too soon, he calls, "No more exploring today, Laddie. Get settled—we're going to be talking for a while."

"How'd all this stuff get here? It's too much to carry on foot the way we came. Besides, the tunnel's way too narrow for some of it to get through."

"Exactly so, I thought you'd spot that. This much treasure couldn't have gotten here even with a lot of helpers."

"Then, how'd you do it?"

"Not all done by me—not by a long shot. It happened over a long stretch. Think of this place as being where two realms touch. On the other side of where we're sitting is fairy country—a whole different reality. Most of this stuff was brought here by way of Fairyland. Right through these rock walls. Not much toting or grunting that way."

"Huh?"

"It's just a different dimension. Both are real, in their way—and not that far apart. And once you figure out how to move easily between them, it's no big trick going from one world to the other. And there are many other dimensional realities besides. You humans only live in one of them and don't have any idea what you're missing."

"If you say so... I cannot speak for other humans, but I'm starting to believe your world is real in ways I don't understand at all. So, I'll take your word for it.

"That's good enough, Laddie, good enough."

Jeep had so many questions he didn't know where to start. "So, what is this place? Why…?"

"You're in the Chamber of Ancient Wisdom, a protective home for irreplaceable treasures from long ago. They bear witness to important conflicts between good and evil that changed the course of the world.

"But what's all this stuff for?"

"What you see here isn't just tons of precious old stuff. Nae, Laddie. This place is sort of like a museum, some items are thousands of years old. Everything brought down here played a role in the never-ending war between the forces of light and the forces of darkness.

"Sometimes good prevails, and sometimes it fails for a time. But the noble efforts of innumerable brave people have managed to keep the power of good from being snuffed out.

"What you see here are reminders of things that matter—like honor and courage. Keeping these treasures in a safe place prevents vital links to ancient times from being forgotten.

"These things you see here aren't merely priceless or beautiful. Each of them has a special energy. You probably noticed that you can feel the powerful binkle energy in this chamber. Everything here is saturated with it. This is a storehouse for binkle power.

"Only a few of those long-ago confrontations between light and dark energies show up in the myths or fairy tales. Much more has been lost to memory—but their existence here keeps a tangible link to what could so easily be forgotten.

"You mean, those mythical battles I've read about really happened?"

"Aye, Laddie. They were real enough at the time, and stay alive in the re-telling. Myth doesn't mean made up. You know. There's a nugget of truth in most of them."

"Wow! How old is this place?"

"Really old. And most of what's in here is even before my time. I'm humbled by all the remarkable heroism that's represented here. They fought for the right and honorable, and they kept that light alive.

"But enough questions, Laddie. Any of us who are still alive and know what's at stake must continue to fight that worthy fight."

Grikkl's eyes mist up with sad memories. He falls silent as a lone tear follows the lattice of wrinkles until it is lost in his bushy white beard. The gnome looks even older than usual, recalling so much of what has been lost.

"Even today?"

"Especially today, Laddie. The stakes are higher than ever. There's much truth to be learned from the old myths and folk tales.

"They speak directly to the emotions. The language of love and the heart. The bravery of those mostly nameless heroes in costly defeats and victories is beyond imagining. These marvelous treasures you see here are just the reminders of their noble sacrifices."

"I'll bet you could tell me a story about everything that's in here," Jeep suggests hopefully.

"That I could, Jeep, that I could... But there won't be time for such things today. Not all the tales are as grand as King Arthur and his knights. And not all these treasures come from mighty battles. Like this here."

Grikkl grabs up a coil of rope. It seems ordinary except for its strange shiny color.

"This rope was made by Hildegarde the Worthy—although she was just plain Hildegarde when she made this. She lived in the mountains of Bavaria, she did—not yet twenty years old.

"About thirty women were being held to compel their village leaders to surrender to an evil band of outlaws. They were imprisoned in a tower overlooking steep and dangerous high mountain cliffs. The women were being slowly starved to death, and they couldn't last much longer.

"Hildegard persuaded all the women to cut off their hair and they worked for days to braid it into this strong rope. The captives used it to get away through the only window in the tower. Their courageous escape inspired the rest of the villagers to stand up to the tyrants and drive them off."

"I'll bet that was a long time ago, wasn't it?"

"Aye, Jeep. Tyrants have been around a long time—but they're still around today, too. And they rely on evil to accomplish what they want. People are suffering terribly because their reprehensible schemes just keep popping up wherever people are most vulnerable.

"But enough history and philosophy. I brought you here for a special reason.

"Is it magic?"

Grikkl smiles his wise and mysterious smile, "Aye. Magic, at least the good kind, certainly can't happen without it. But it's more like energy—a special kind of energy."

"I'm not following you."

"That's because you can't understand what I'm talking about— not with the head, anyway. It's something you have to feel here." He pats his heart. "When you're able to feel this energy yourself, the rest of what I'm saying will make more sense to you. Still, today you start to understand something big—and small at the same time."

Grikkl absent-mindedly strokes his beard before asking, "What do you know about atoms, Jeep?"

"My class spent a week studying atoms. They're extremely tiny, but everything you can touch is made out of them."

"That's right Laddie. But the energy that comes from atoms has immense power—more power than you'd suspect from their teeny size. What I'm talking about, the binkle power accumulated in this chamber, is a lot like atomic energy—small but powerful. Once you know what you're looking for, you are able to recognize signs of that power everywhere.

"See all those paintings over there? What they show played a part in bringing more binkle energy into the world, too. Binkles and beauty go together. Since binkles can happen whenever a person is touched by something beautiful, it's often found in the natural beauty of the outdoors. Or you can find them in any of the arts—like in music, and paintings, and dance, and poetry.

"Great art touches a person deeply because some artists are skilled enough to capture the binkle energy in what they make. Through their art other people can actually feel the energy that inspired their creation."

Jeep was used to Grikkl saying little, but that day Grikkl spoke for a long time without a break. Jeep didn't follow all of what Grikkl told him. But he could tell the gnome was revealing secrets known only to a few.

Grikkl finally stops talking, and the silence grows as long as the shadows around the rock walls.

Jeep timidly asks, "Why are you telling all this to me?"

"Because you already used this energy. But you need to understand it better."

"How could I? I just found out about it."

"Jeep, you used its power when you called out to me that night I brought you home."

"When you found me? You must be mistaken. I was helpless. I did nothing."

Grikkl erupts. "Nothing?! Indeed! Don't be silly! You summoned magic to your aid. It was weak. But I felt it and the animals felt it, too."

"No way! I couldn't have! I don't know how. I'll admit, I tried. I made a wish but it didn't change anything."

"And I'm telling you it did! You foolish lad. You called me to you. I was obligated to respond to your summons. And there was no doubt magic was at work."

"You felt that…? I guess I have to believe you, but how?" *But I couldn't have. That makes no sense at all.*

"Aye Laddie, I felt the urgency of your summons. I had to come—no question about that. What I didn't know was whether it was dark power or light power you were using."

"You must have decided I'm OK, or you wouldn't have brought me home."

"Exactly so, Laddie. Once I checked you over good and proper I could tell you were a good 'un. Rough around the edges, but you'll be learnin' with time."

Grikkl's face and bearing indicate a shift to more serious matters. "There's more to tell you later, but today I have to warn you. You're returning home soon, so you have to be ready."

"Ready? For what?"

"There are risks... You must become more careful—more watchful for dangers. Once someone knows about what you know, you could become a threat to them."

"I'm just a kid. I'm not a threat to anybody. Besides, who...?"

Grikkl waives Jeep's protest away. "Believe me, there are evil people who want this knowledge to stay lost—forever. To destroy these precious objects and what they stand for.

"As you learn how to use more binkle power, they'll notice you. You could be in peril. But until you're smarter about how to control the full force of binkle energy, you won't know how to use it for your protection."

Jeep thinks a moment. "Can't you protect me? Maybe I should stay here with you and Adah..."

"That's not your answer. Your own power can protect you— once you've learned how to listen to it."

"Then teach me."

Grikkl sits back and smiles, his wise eyes twinkling, "As you wish. As you wish."

"I'm ready."

"Then I need to show you something, something you can take with you."

Grikkl opens a very old wooden chest. He squats down on the floor so he can and rummage through the lowest drawer. A grunt of satisfaction announces he'd found what he's looking for. He straightens up again.

"Catch, Laddie!" as Grikkl tosses the object at the startled boy.

Jeep snags it out of the air, then studies the item carefully. He holds a gold medallion—about 1¼ inches across and worn smooth in places. There's a round hole near the edge, so it could hang.

One side shows a hopping rabbit that reminded him of Lulu. On the other is a symbol Jeep doesn't recognize.

"There's great power in this talisman— made even stronger because of Lulu's affectionate bond with you. Before you go home, I'll show you how it works."

Jeep grins as he holds the ancient charm against his chest. It seems to pulse with energy. "I can almost feel its magic."

"Aye, Laddie, that you can. Magic that can help protect you. But more on that another day. Now it's time for us to go."

Jeep helps Grikkl carry his manuscripts back through the tunnel. Jeep's mind is discombobulated by all the strange things he has seen and heard in the Chamber.

So, he follows along behind Grikkl and Cerberus like a person in a trance.

CHAPTER 6
JEEP DISCOVERS YOU
CAN GO HOME AGAIN

Grikkl said, "Jeep, you need to know that what you've been eating, the faduki, isn't ordinary food."

"I've figured that out—and I like the way it tastes a lot better."

"That's not what I'm talking about. It doesn't just taste different. It changes the way your body works. Adah and I have eaten it for centuries, but you're not used to it. You'll start to feel its side effects before long. A steady diet of it probably wouldn't do you any harm—but it will affect your ears."

"My ears are fine."

"Listen, Jeep, you're not hearing me! I'm trying to tell you something new, something important."

Just then, Lulu hops over and rubs her whole self against Jeep's leg. He lifts her up and takes a long moment to stroke her fur against his cheek, before she settles into his arms.

Once Jeep returns his attention to Grikkl, he notices an odd expression on the gnome's wrinkled face.

"I see. You're able to hear Lulu far better than you can hear me—since hers is the language of affection. No question but

Lulu says more to you than I can. She speaks directly to your heart."

Then Grikkl adds with a laugh, "But don't be surprised to find she speaks to you in other ways as well."

During Jeep's stay, Grikkl spent most of his time working at the table forever piled high with a constantly changing assortment of books and papers. Grikkl ignored everything else going on, so Jeep and Adah were careful not to distract him.

Now and then, Grikkl grunts in annoyance or satisfaction as he combs through them. But other than that, he hardly made a sound.

Old books and rolled-up parchments are piled in every unused area of the floor, making it tricky to get around without tripping over them. Most are written in a language Jeep doesn't recognize. And the notes Grikkl scribbles use those same cryptic characters.

As his energy returns, Jeep explores the gnomes' home. The hollowed-rock cavern is compact. Yet it doesn't feel crowded—even though it lacks windows or a view. Another smaller room, where Grikkl and Adah sleep, is filled to the ceiling with stacked barrels and crates. No telling what's in there.

Both rooms are made cheerful with colorful cushions and blankets that Adah had knitted herself. And beautiful tapestries that probably came from the Chamber hang on the walls.

Jeep drew a simple map because making maps was second nature to him.

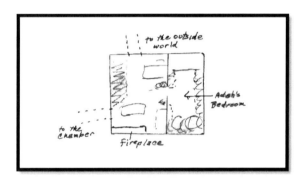

Since she first sang the mermaid's song for him, Jeep felt emotionally drawn to be with Adah. For her part, she is quick to hug him close in her wide, welcoming arms. But she's so short the hugs are on the low side—unless he's sitting down. He never resists her spur-of-the-moment warmth. *I missed hugs for too long. At last I'm wanted again.*

Sometimes Adah recounted amazing tales of long ago, full of dash and excitement. Jeep can't tell whether she's talking about her own experiences or repeating ancient yarns. Although he assumes her stories about fairies, elves, and unicorns have to be made up, Adah speaks of them as if they are personal friends of hers.

Adah fills in more details about what Grikkl already told him in the Chamber. She ends with, "I want to be sure you'll be ready."

That word again. I don't know what I'm getting ready for.

"Ready—for what?"

"You'll see."

"That's not a good enough answer," he objects. "How in the world am I supposed to get ready when you and Grikkl only talk in riddles?"

"But a riddle's only perplexing until you figure it out. You will—I'm sure of it." Her confiding wink stops further complaint.

Every time Adah gives him more binkle advice, Jeep would jot it down:

   - When you're not quite sure what to do, just stop and ask yourself, "Do I want a binkle or something else?" Unless you *really* want a binkle you'll probably just get any old thing.

   - Binkles get passed along in all sorts of ways, by a smile or a firm handshake—and especially a hug.

   - Children are the very best of all at finding binkles— everywhere they look.

- Don't feel bad if you forget about them
sometimes. Maybe the next time you'll want the
binkle more—enough to stay alert for them.

- Look for the energy zizz any time during the day,
especially while other things are going on. It's mighty easy to
tune them out.

- A binkle is a heart giggle. It wipes out the glums.

Jeep listens to her advice but doesn't find it very helpful. *It's
too perplexing. She acts like what she tells me makes this binkle stuff
all clear— when it doesn't. It's just more riddles on top of riddles.*

Another time, Adah told him, "If you want to find your own
powers you must listen from another place—inside. You must
learn to trust the still small voice."

"Whose voice?"

"Why, the voice of your own wisdom. Everyone has a voice
of wisdom—but it takes a special kind of listening."

Jeep makes a disbelieving face. She didn't argue except to
say, "If you're able to hear my wisdom, you can hear your
own as well. They might even sound alike, once in a while."

He starts to say he doesn't know how. But Adah puts her
finger on his lips and smiles. "Jeep, I know you can find
your own wisdom…. And you'll find that you like to, too."

So, he holds his tongue, while never quite believing he
can do what she wants.

Jeep's favorite song that Adah sings is "The Song of Birds." He can't get her to sing it often enough to suit him, since it takes him to a wonderful place.

I can't believe I'm not a bird flying through the air—gliding, and swooping, and landing. It feels so real! Soaring high above leafy green trees and gardens, or snuggled into my tight-woven nest that's perched way out on a narrow branch, I even feel the warmth of the sun on my outstretched wings.

As Adah sings that song, scraps of birdsong fill Jeep's head—joyous chirps, clucks, warbles and thrums. The sensations of a bird's life are so lifelike to him that Jeep is sure he can think like a bird.

While still in that "birdhead," Jeep wanders over to Ramses.

"Schz," Ramses screeches at him.

Jeep tries to repeat the sound, "Schlarg?"

"Schz."

"Scrag?" said Jeep.

"Schz," Ramses screeches at him. "Schz, schz."

"Schhhz" gets closer.

"Schz!" Ramses impatiently spits it out again. "Schz…"

Jeep jumps. He shakes his head and rubs his ear. *That's strange!*

"Schz," repeats the bird, even louder.

"I heard you! I know what you said!" ("Hello, good looking" in bird talk.) Ramses nods his whole body in approval—like the forward-and-back motion of a rocking horse.

Jeep feels a thrill of excitement from head to toe. *Ohmygosh, it is magic! I can do magic too! I knew it! I knew it! It's not just something to read about—or that Grikkl and Adah do. It happened to me! I always wanted it to be true—now I know I was right!*

When Jeep realizes he is soon to go home, he urges Adah, "Can't I stay here? I hate to leave you and all your magic. I wish my home could be like this."

"But Jeep, don't you know that there's as much magic in your world as there is here? It's there, honest."

"You've gotta be crazy. There is no magic—none!"

She grins patiently. "Grikkl and I are sending you back home so you can learn to recognize the magic that exists in your everyday life. Once you can spot it you can plug into it any time you want."

"It's not there, Adah. I'd have noticed."

Again, that patient smile of hers. "The trick comes from knowing how to spot it—how to *feel its presence*, actually. Since the energy of magic *is* there.

"If you want to find magic in the making, you've got to spot its signs *while it's happening*. Once you learn how to sense its presence, you need to keep noticing that feeling so it keeps right on happening."

Grikkl has been listening and jumps in. "Harrumph, Adah's right, you know. There's magic that's all grand and glorious—but mostly that's tricks just put on for show. Don't pay too much attention to that stuff.

"Real power is tiny—really tiny, so small you can barely feel it. But it's worth your noticing because that kind is real. Sure, there's magical energy down here, but there's plenty of it to be found in your human world as well.

"I don't expect you to see very much of it yet. It's there, though. And, sooner or later, you'll discover it where you least expect to find it."

Adah presses a cluster of yellow flowers picked from her fresh-as-a-garden dress into Jeep's hand. "These blossoms will remind you that magic is real—if you choose to see it."

She also places a generous package of faduki cookies in his hands. "Eat several of these every day until we see you again. They'll make you stronger—in ways that make it possible for you to get back here."

Adah hugs him goodbye for an extra-long time, and he dreads leaving them. She whispers in a confiding way, "You do know that what's special between you and me is binkles, don't you? If you ever forget that feeling just think about me or Lulu. You'll get a tiny *zizz* of it again."

 "I suppose so—but I'd rather be here with you."

"True, I'd like that, too. But now it's time for you to discover how to get that feeling with many other people. Anytime, anywhere you find yourself. I know you can, Jeep."

"I'm not good around people."

"It doesn't matter. You can do it—and more besides." She raises her hand to block his objections. "I sense your worry. You've hit a rough patch because your mother's ill. But you have enough power to handle whatever difficulties come along. More than enough. You'll see that binkles can help you deal with your problems back home."

Jeep pulls away and can only wince inside. *She doesn't understand. I just can't...* But words do not come to explain his sorrow. "If you say so." Jeep shrugs and makes a face. *I'd like it to be true—but... I just feel so helpless.*

Lulu sticks to Jeep like Velcro. She wants nothing beyond nestling in his lap as he strokes her ears. One day when she's nestled in his lap, Jeep thinks he almost hears a wee, tinny voice.

"Pay attention, Jeep."

"Huh? Who's that?" He swings his head around quickly, but he doesn't see anyone.

"I said, pay attention," the voice repeats with more force. Once more, Jeep looks around. Nobody is there—again.

"Cut it out! It's me—Lulu," says the same squeaky voice.

Jeep is so startled he leaps up without thinking and drops her.

"Lulu…? You can talk?"

It's got to be my imagination. I don't know how to understand her. He stares at her lips to see if they move.

"Sure, silly. Of course, you're hearing me."

"This is a trick, and not a very good one."

"No tricks."

"It's the magic of this place, right? It makes you seem to be talking."

"No, it's *you!*"

"How could it be me? I never heard you speak before."

"That's true. The faduki does it. Eating it started to change your ears. Gnomes naturally understand what animals say, but the faduki lets you understand us, too."

"You're telling me I can hear other animals besides you?"

"Most of them—if you try. You'll get better at it once you practice."

"Great! Not just you?"

Cerberus stretches and yawns with his cavernous jaws before drawling, "It's no big deal, you know. Us animals can always talk to each other. I'd say you've been kind of slow to catch on. Humans aren't as smart as they think they are."

Jeep can understand the dog's words as well. *I can't decide whether or not I've been insulted. But heck, I really don't care.*

He is speechless in either language—just holding Lulu all the closer.

"Grikkl, I don't want to go back. I like it here with you and Adah. Chris is gonna be really mad. Except for MeToo, nobody cares whether I'm home or not."

Grikkl makes a ridiculous, silly face at the frowning boy that brings forth a mild chuckle. But Grikkl will not budge. "There's no other choice. It's time for you to test your wings."

"I don't want to go," Jeep insists. But Grikkl ignores any further protests.

"While almost everybody can and does binkle sometimes, they don't *know they can*. And they don't do it on purpose. You do—that by itself, counts as a big deal."

Grikkl wags his finger at Jeep and grins as he adds, "Besides, you're able to do even more."

"Yeah? Like what?"

"That's what you will discover. You have to find binkles all by yourself out there in the normal world. We've talked about this, remember? The zizz."

"I get it. But that doesn't mean I agree."

"Even though you can return here, 'here' is hard to describe. It won't show on any map. This place is protected to keep it hidden from negative energy. Back home you must find ways to supply your own binkle energy.

"Unless you can sustain enough of it yourself, you won't have enough to be able to get back to us. Is that clear?"

Grikkl's stern manner sends an icy chill through Jeep's body. "I have to come back—I have to! Tell me what to do."

"You must wait at least ten days before returning. It could be even longer if you're short of binkle power. Is that clear?"

Jeep nods. "Ten days, but no more. I'll find a way."

"Good lad. Here's your ticket."

Grikkl helps Jeep attach his rabbit medallion to a leather cord and fastens it around the boy's neck.

"I placed another strong return spell on it. When you're ready to come back, hold this gold piece against your chest with both hands and think intensely about Lulu. That activates the love-bond spell. You two are linked together with heart energy. So, you'll be carried back here through forces I can't explain to you yet.

"I can do that. I can!"

"I never doubted that you could. And Adah doesn't doubt it either."

"One last thing you need to know. The intense binkle energy around here creates a curious distortion. Time and space don't act the same way you're used to. When you get home, you'll find almost no time has passed since you left. I doubt anyone will even notice you've been gone."

"That would be great—if it works," says an unconvinced Jeep.

Grikkl grins mysteriously and winks at him. "I'm sending you back to your own bed on the very same night you arrived. All will be well.

"As you step back into the life you already know, remember— you're not the same as you were before. Many things you're used to will feel strange now."

The last words are Grikkl's, but Jeep's last thoughts are about Lulu. She rubs her silken fur against him as she beams loving devotion…

And that's apparently what Jeep dreams about. For the next thing he remembers, he wakes up with a contented smile— and in his own bed.

His fingers reach up to stroke the worn metal of the medallion hanging from his neck. *Oh yes, it happened!* And he knows he hasn't just dreamed the whole thing.

MeToo jumps all over him as he stirs. The dog's energetic affection makes Jeep glad to be back.

"Oh, MeToo—I sure have missed you. How'd you find your way home?"

In reply, the dog just wags his tail from his neck on back, and slobbers all over Jeep's hands.

Jeep turns on the TV news and discovers he hasn't lost any days after all. (*Grikkl was right!*) He dresses for school, just like any other day. Chris doesn't notice anything is out of the ordinary.

As Jeep eats his cereal, the already-patched leg of his kitchen chair breaks. He barely saves himself from falling to the floor. But the jerk makes him spill milk all over the table, and he has to clean it up.

"Well, things are just the same around here," Jeep mumbles with annoyance. Then he packs a lunch, gathers up his books, and heads off to school.

CHAPTER 7
ASK NOT FOR WHOM
THE BULLY WAITS

Jeep hurries to catch up with Louise and Anna, classmates who live down the block. The sisters look enough alike to be twins—blue eyes, brown pigtails, and pale skin splashed with freckles. Their thoughts are so in tune that either could finish her sister's sentences. A year older, Louise looks after Anna, who gets easily upset.

The sisters are the only people Jeep knows who love reading even more than he does. So, their conversation is usually sprinkled with talk about books they liked.

"Hey, Jeep, where you been?" Anna calls.

How could she know? Caught by surprise, Jeep tells a boldface lie. "What do you mean? I didn't go anywhere." *This better not make my nose grow.*

"Oh yes, you did! Didn't he, Louise?"

Louise looks him in the eye. "So, what's going on? Why'd you try to trick us?"

"Trick you? Why would I do that?" he asks innocently.

"That's what we want to know. Now 'fess up."

"Are you guys saying you missed me?" *Maybe someone cared I was away after all.*

"Sure did!" said both girls with a single voice.

Zizz... I felt that! Just a little one, but I know what it means!

"Really? You really missed me?"

"Cut that out, Jeep! Of course, we missed you! What's this nonsense about?"

"Where were you, and why'd you try to trick us?" Louise adds.

"Well, I was away..., but I wasn't really." *No, that wasn't it.*

Jeep starts over again, "Well, I was gone, but it didn't take any time."

There's no way to explain what really happened—at least so it's believable. Heck, I can hardly believe it myself. And I was there.

Both girls scrunch their faces in puzzlement. "Come again? That doesn't make any sense," said Louise.

"Look, I want to tell you, but it's kind of complicated. Way complicated... Can't we talk about it after school?"

"After school, then. And you'd better cut out this game you're playing," Anna insists.

Jeep nods. "OK, after school then."

If they can tell I was gone then maybe the time warp doesn't work on them. So, it probably won't hurt to tell them a little. I badly want to tell somebody. Zizz...

Nothing that happens during Jeep's school day went quite the way it usually did. He knows he's different somehow, although he can't exactly put it into words. The teachers and other students treat him the same as always—which means they ignore him.

But on the inside, Jeep doesn't feel like he's the same person everybody thinks he is anymore. It's as if he's wearing a disguise—but *disguised as himself*. And no one seems to notice that difference.

Jeep treats every word or gesture that's directed at him as if it conveys secret meanings. A glance from a classmate (that he wouldn't have noticed before) sets him wondering. *Are they trying to tell me something? Should I let on?*

Several times, he senses a tiny *zizz*, like when Sue Bickford, who sits in front of him, asks him for his help with a math problem. Or when Mrs. Acton, his teacher, singles out his book report as a first-rate example in front of the whole class.

More than once he catches himself smiling—without intending to.

As Jeep, Anna, and Louise start walking home later, the sidewalk is blocked by Merve, Todd, and Andy. They are a rowdy crew of sixth graders who like to pick on the younger kids. Even the other sixth graders take pains to avoid being pestered by them.

Merve is the ring-leader, but any of them could get an "A" for meanness.

Andy yells at them, "Here comes the freakazoid freckle sisters."

Merve adds, "Yea, there's the creepy girl who can't even talk right."

"L-l-leave me al-l-lone!" Anna pleads.

"Go away, you jerks," Louise counters.

"Now, why'd we want to do that?" Merve asks with a singsong voice. "You weirdoes should be glad we let you pass at all, especially th-th-the weird one."

"S-s-cram y-y-you…"

"You guys are jerks…" Louise starts to say, but Todd knocks her down mid-sentence. Then all three boys run off laughing.

Jeep is madder at himself than at the bullies. *I didn't even try to help. What kind of friend does that make me?*

The three of them walk the rest of the way in silent gloom. The ugly business has dampened their spirits.

As they near home, the three of them sit down in the grass and start talking about where Jeep went. Jeep describes his fall and the cold, miserable night in the woods when it all started.

I guess it's OK to tell a little—as long as I don't mention the Chamber of Ancient Wisdom. After all, a promise is a promise.

The sisters are hungry for every detail about the wise old gnomes—their wrinkled-up faces that almost twinkle as they talk, their old-fashioned clothes, and even the way they shimmer when the light seems to pass through them.

Jeep describes Nelda, Lulu, and every one of the animals with enough specific details and stories for Anna and Louise to see them in their mind's eye. He even shows them the map he'd drawn of the gnome home.

Jeep isn't the least bit successful in explaining Adah's songs since they have no tunes—or words. Even while they created a mood that was as real as could be.

Yet the girls understand how deeply he'd been touched by Adah's singing. He even repeated several of Grikkl's stories.

Jeep fears that his report might sound too much like make believe. *I might just as well tell the truth. If they don't believe it, too bad. Even I've got to admit it sounds made up.*

But neither girl doubts a word he tells them, or considers it too farfetched. They just wish they could've been there too.

But about the Chamber of Ancient Wisdom or the binkle Jeep breathes not a word.

As he finishes, Jeep asks Louise how come she could tell he was away.

"I couldn't tell how long you were gone. I only knew that you were *away from me*, like we got disconnected. But that's over now."

Anna adds, "Same here. Something was missing. That's why I'm glad you're back."

Although Jeep already was friendly with the sisters before his adventure, they had never been as close as he feels to them right then. *I want to trust them. I like feeling missed.*

In unguarded moments, Jeep sometimes wonders if his time with the gnomes might've just been something he dreamed up. But those doubts never last long. He only needs to touch or smell Adah's magic flowers (that still looked freshly picked) stuck in a small bottle on his desk.

One sniff and the memories rush back. *I know Adah is every bit as real as these flowers.*

Each morning, Jeep eats two magic cookies as he counts down the days. *I can return in nine days… then eight…, then seven…,* Just that thought of getting back to Lulu and Adah brings a happy *zizz*.

Each faduki cookie is such a treat that he stretches out eating it as long as he can. He thinks about his choice—mentally tasting each possibility. *Let's see, what am I in the mood for? Lemon cream pie? Cherry tarts? A juicy burger?*

102

He even tried green eggs and ham—that only sounds bad, but tastes OK.

Once, after eating part of his cookie (triple-cheese and sausage pizza), Jeep changes his mind, preferring the sweetness of a strawberry milkshake. The next mouthful tastes exactly like that. *Two tastes from one cookie—not bad. How about three?*

But once the newness wore off, Jeep decides to specialize—in chocolate. After studying several cookbooks, he makes a list of 83 chocolate dishes he wants. He intends to work his way through the list—and then start over:

Chocolate mousse
Chocolate parfait
Chocolate brownies
Chocolate layer cake
Chocolate macaroons
Chocolate-mint sundae
Chocolate truffles (That one is a surprise. It doesn't have any truffles in it, and it wouldn't taste great if it did.)

And so on…

Still, in most regards Jeep's life at home isn't any better than before. His stepfather is hardly ever home since he holds down two jobs.

During the week, he works in the office of a mattress factory (and would repeat the same old joke, "There's no lying down on the job").

Four nights a week he works as second cook at a diner. When he is at home, Chris is always tired—too tired for doing much with Jeep. Besides, they'd never been all that close.

They only spoke about the daily matters—sign the report card; we're out of milk; remember to put out the trash. They didn't talk—let alone do much of anything away from home together.

Jeep is so tired of them never having money to do anything fun that he'd given up asking.

Jeep is stuck doing almost all the housework, plus the truffle chores. Doing dishes, laundry, and all the rest isn't that difficult for him. And he actually likes the cooking part, since he used to do so much of that with his mother.

They puttered around in the kitchen making meals together. She'd tell him that when she was a girl no bigger than him, her grandmother taught her to make this very same recipe (like her famous ginger snaps) that she is teaching him to make now.

Cooking is funny too since she insisted upon never doing things the same way twice. So, there would sometimes be some strange results— especially if they were baking. The failures that were truly inedible she sacrificed to the "habit gods.

As they cooked together, Jeep would tell her his dreams for the future, and faraway places he wanted to visit someday. And she told about her hopes and dreams as well.

Cooking isn't mainly about fixing food—it's about being close, doing things together. That's what I miss the most since she left—the sharing parts. Nowadays, cooking is just about making things to eat.

Sometimes Chris brings leftovers from the diner where he works. He and Chris get by OK, but mealtime isn't special any more.

Day after day, Merve's crew singles out Anna and Louise for their cruel mischief—chasing them and calling them hurtful names: Freckleface, Stupid lips, Fritterhead.

Just knowing they might be waiting fills Anna with dread. Long before the final school bell rings, she's scared to go home.

Those fears made her stutter even worse. Her teacher, Miss Pringle, warns her, "Anna, where *is* your mind wandering off to? Start paying attention."

Being criticized in front of the class just upsets her more. She chews her lips and tries to hold her tears back. Not always successfully.

Louise watches Anna's misery, but has no idea how to protect her. The mean boys weren't afraid of anything she can do to them. If anything, sticking up for Anna just makes them nastier.

Jeep stands by helplessly. Merve's crew ignores him, and even the sisters don't act like he'd be much help to them. *I'm tired of letting my friends down. I need to make a stand somehow.*

Helen's absence is hard for Chris too. He works himself to weariness and drags himself home. Their apartment has become a place without love, and they both badly miss her.

I assumed Chris works so hard because we need the money. But maybe he dreads coming home without her being here.

Jeep hates Chris keeping him in the dark about how his mom is getting along. He finally works up his courage and demands to know, "Why won't you ever tell me about her? Isn't she getting better? Can't I go see her?"

Chris answers like he always did, "I don't want to talk about it now."

"I know you don't. But I want to see her, you know. I'm old enough."

"No! It's a bad idea."

"But I need to know…"

Chris hisses, "Boy, you don't want to know! You don't want to see her like that!"

"Like what?"

"Nothing. Just forget it."

"But doesn't she miss me, too?"

"No! She doesn't miss anything—or anyone. She's gone. Get used to the idea."

"But she's alive. You see her. Why can't you take me with you?"

"She's out of her head. And there's nothing you or I can do about it."

"No. You're wrong!"

Mom's sick, but that doesn't make her crazy. But if Chris thinks so, that could explain why she never wrote to me, not even once. No—I don't believe it. Not my mom.

"Oh Jeep, I wish I were." Chris rambles on, talking more to himself than to the boy. "You think you're the only one who misses her? Nobody ever loved me like she did—nobody. Now she's gone off her head, and who knows if she'll ever be back."

"I still want to see her. She needs to know I still love her..."

"Like that's going to do her any good. I tell you, you don't want to see her!"

"Please... I have to go."

"No, it's final. I'm doing what's best. Though I know you won't thank me for it."

Chris stomps from the room. So, with bitterness between them, the man and the boy go to bed, each feeling his lonely sorrow.

Since his return from Grikkl's, Jeep looks and acts pretty much the same as ever—on the outside. He was never much of a talker and rather skillful at avoiding attention. *Sure, I've got opinions, doesn't everyone? But I try to keep them to myself.*

Jeep's adventure underground didn't change that. Jeep still felt as awkward as ever talking about himself or what he thinks.

But on the inside, he doesn't feel the same about anything. *I know something really important! And no one else does.*

Sometimes his new attitude about getting binkles makes him forget to be standoffish.

Jeep cannot bear the thought that he won't get back to Grikkl's soon. But as the gnomes had warned him, his return requires lots of binkles. And it's up to him to figure out how.

At first, he just wants to get binkles as easily as he can. But when he just hangs around happy and laughing people, expecting to soak them up, he doesn't end up with many. It's like catching snowflakes with your tongue—that's a mighty slow way to get a drink.

I remember Adah saying that if you give binkles to other people, you're more likely to get some, too.

So, Jeep stays alert for situations where people are having fun—which requires him being in groups of people, something that he previously avoided. Being with them involves a certain amount of smiling and acting like he's terribly interested in what they're talking about.

It starts with him *pretending to care*. But before long, Jeep discovers he means it—more often than not. Somehow, even a particle of sincerity changes the way people respond to him— and vice versa.

When a *zizz* comes at such times, he notices that he really is enjoying himself. And other people present are enjoying his participation as well. Jeep got enough good energy from those initial experiments to consider other changes that could speed his binkle collecting up.

He decides to stop eating lunch by himself. With his tray in hand, Jeep looks around at the knots of students in the cafeteria. He doesn't feel drawn to join any of them. Instead, he prefers to sit down next to someone sitting all alone.

Trevor is a new kid in his grade who Jeep hardly knows. The two smile at each other timidly, then exchange a few words. But they soon discover they share an interest in adventure stories. Then there was no stopping the flood of "Did you

read…? And
"What about that escape…?"

Lunch was over too quickly. But not before they binkled plenty, and know there'll be more lunches together to come.

The next day, Jeep eats lunch with Cindy, who is sitting by herself. The other students tease her about being a fatso. Once the two of them get past an awkward start, Cindy tells him about growing up in far-away lands, where her military father was posted.

Her descriptions of the foods in Germany, the exotic daily routines of Korea, and the haunting beauty of the Asian forests make Jeep ache to go there. Binkles came fast for Jeep and Cindy. *I'm breaking habits and won't be able to think of myself as shy anymore. Zizz…*

Jeep soon learns that even the briefest activity can bring a binkle back—without a word being exchanged. Like the time he smiled at the clerk the whole time she rang up his grocery purchase.

As she hands over his change, with smiling eyes she pauses long enough to enjoy the moment of sincere connection too.

Zizz… And whatdoyaknow! She passes that happy energy along to the next three customers behind him. Each one beamed.

So, Jeep can recognize slight ways he's changing from the way he was before. Not big things, not so anyone else would notice for sure—but he could.

Feeling unsure of himself wasn't such a heavy weight as it used to be. He knew a binkle would make that yuccy feeling vanish for a while. And somehow, not as many things seemed scary anymore.

CHAPTER 8
LAUGHTER AT THE ZOO

One day after school, Louise challenges Jeep and Anna, "Why don't we go to the zoo today. I've got free passes—even coupons for ice cream."

"Can we have chocolate?" Jeep asks.

"You and chocolate," said Louise as she rolls her eyes. "Don't you ever get enough?"

"Enough? I can't imagine what enough chocolate would be like. Would that be like enough money or enough time?"

"Or enough clothes, or enough rides on a roller coaster?" asks Anna.

"That's too much thinking. We're here for fun," insists Louise, with a laugh. The friends are soon strolling through Truman Zoo. They see signs of disorder all over the place. Several popular exhibits are closed to the public.

Large signs announce the entire zoo will be closed starting on a particular date—without any indication of how soon it would re-open. Louise asks an employee what' going on.

He tells her "A large factory is going to be built nearby. All that construction racket at will disturb the animals. Most of them are being moved as far from the noise as we can put them. But we've run out of places for them to go."

"Too bad," Anna replies. "That's going to crowd the exhibits even worse."

"It can't be good for the animals," Louise adds.

"No, but what choice do we have?" the workman shrugs.

The friends start at the Monkey House. Monkeys aren't too proud to act like silly clowns to keep peoples' attention. The friends watch their antics with pleasure until they notice several young monkeys picking on at a smaller one.

Louise grumbles, "Oh no, I wish they wouldn't do that. I came here to forget about bullies."

"That's mean! Can't we stop them?" Anna asks. But they can't do much about the bad treatment from outside the bars.

Jeep tries to understand the chatter coming from inside the monkey cage. But the situation can be grasped easily, just from watching their behavior.

Without pausing to think, Jeep lets loose a mouthful of scrambled sounds. What he says makes no sense to bystanders. But to the two mean monkeys it sounds like, "I'm going to tell your mother!"

That's bad news for misbehaving offspring—human or monkey. Deserting their mischief, the mean monkeys scamper away.

The picked-on one swings arm over arm along the bars until he reaches Jeep. Then it jabbers at him. Just from the tone and gestures alone, Jeep recognizes a thank you.

Anna and Louise look stunned by what just happened. Louise asks, "What was that all about? How did you learn to speak monkey talk?"

"I really can't," Jeep protests.

"But we heard you..." the girls say with one voice.

"It's not what you think."

"Just fill us in and we'll decide what to think for ourselves," says Anna.

"Sorry I didn't mention it but I'm not very good. Cerberus makes fun of my animal talk every chance. Even though I'm getting better, it still seems like a foreign language to me."

At the girls' prompting, Jeep describes his brief, unexpected exchanges with Ramses and Lulu.

"It's another effect from me eating faduki every day. Who knows if there could be more effects I haven't noticed yet."

Anna answers, "Well Jeep, here's the best place to practice. We want to watch …"

Louise breaks in, "I dare you. I double dare you to make a lion laugh. Do you think you can?"

"Or a bear or a snake," says Anna. "Let's say we cannot go home until you make at least two animals laugh at what you say. Deal?"

By now, both Anna and Louise are laughing uproariously at the idea of Jeep being a comedian for animals. There's no way for Jeep to get out of it.

If I've got to do it, I might as well be as silly as possible.

Jeep askes a zebra, "Do you have time to hear a joke?"

The zebra replies, "You're not going to try that embarrassed zebra joke on me, are you?"

[*Old version—What's black and white and read all over? Answer: A newspaper - New version—What's black and white and red all over? Answer: An embarrassed zebra*]

"Certainly not. I wouldn't insult you with that old relic. It's apparent you're much too witty for that."

"I thought I'd offer you a 'Get Out of Jail Free' card."

"Why's that?"

116

"Well, they've got you locked up in there. But the keeper said you can go free—if you change your stripes."

The zebra groans, turns, and trots off.

Jeep asks Anna, "Doesn't a groan count? He got my joke, even though he didn't like it."

"Half score then. I'll expect you to do better with the snakes." Finding a snake that would even talk to him turns out to be pretty tough. Snakes have no interest whatsoever in being sociable.

When Jeep gets a large rattlesnake to listen, he asks, "Do you do much reading?"

To which the snake replies, "I'd have a little trouble turning the pages, don't you think? Besides, what's worth reading?"

"I've heard that Snakespeare is pretty popular," Jeep says, without blowing his punch line.

Not getting a laugh, he keeps on going. "What do you get when you cross a snake and a kangaroo?"

The snake doesn't know or care, but only waves his head around when Jeep replies, "A jump rope." Still no laugh.

The snake takes charge, "Let me ask you one. What did Noah give the animals who couldn't get on the ark?"

Jeep doesn't know. When the snake answers, "A rain check," he chuckles.

Jeep asks Anna, "Do I get any points if the animals get me to laugh?"

She makes a face. "Don't make me laugh."

Jeep tried again, "What do snakes study in school? (hisstory), to which the snake rolls his eyes. "I hear snakes don't have basements in their houses." He pauses for drama, "They only have crawl spaces."

The snake rewards him with a reluctant guffaw.

Anna announces, "OK, that one's a full point. Now you have one and a half."

By comparison, the polar bear is easy. Jeep asks one, "What do lady polar bears use on their faces at night?"

It probably was a girl bear since it acts embarrassed not to know.

When Jeep says, "*Very* cold cream (beauty cream)," the bear grins, but stops short of a snicker.

Jeep immediately follows with, "Where do pigs live?" Once again, the bear is stumped.

"In a high Grime area," makes her burst into giggles.

"You know," the polar bear remarks, "there's not much dirt where I come from. That's probably why we see so few pigs in the Arctic."

"Another point then," say Anna.

Whereupon, Jeep turns toward the girls and makes a dramatic gesture with his arms. "Da da!" Both girls applaud with gusto.

After so much laughing, the friends eat their ice cream and head toward home in a light-hearted mood.

Jeep tells them, "Since we've all been feeling them this whole time, I guess it's time to tell you about the binkle."

"Dinkle?" asks Louise, "Sounds weird."

"Binkle, with a 'B'—weird but wonderful. Just listen."

So, Jeep finally tells the sisters what the gnomes taught him about binkles. About how to create energy through connecting with other people.

Of course, the sisters understand at once. When it comes to friendship and binkles they are already experts.

The hour is late and Jeep has been asleep for hours. Chris sits at the kitchen table with all his bills sorted into three tidy stacks—pay now, pay a little, put off a bit longer. The third pile is the largest and it seems to grow month by month.

Most of the bills came with fancy "Pay Now" or "Past Due" stickers. Chris can't blame them—but he can't do anything about it, either. He dreads the collection calls that rudely press him for payment. As an honest person, Chris hates that his word isn't considered trustworthy.

Chris got into this fix rather suddenly after Helen's illness. Everything was going along fine while his wife was home. Their combined salaries covered the bills, with enough left over to save toward their own home. Then Helen's medical bills sucked those savings up, and he couldn't keep up.

That's when Chris took a second job. Besides his less-than-satisfying sales job at the mattress factory, most nights he works as a short-order cook, dragging himself home at 10:00. He is always exhausted and a bit foggy.

He cut every expense he could, and watches where each dollar goes. Extras are out of the question. Fortunately, Jeep didn't want much or complain about doing without.

Chris has always been so-so with money. When he was single, he didn't make much, but he didn't spend much either. Once married, Helen handled their finances. She had a knack for it. There always was enough to go around, with some for fun and a bit put aside for a rainy day. This money pinch is yet another reminder why he misses her so much.

At the thought of her, Chris rolls his eyes to the ceiling and groans, "Oh, Helen, it's tough. But I could hang on if I only knew you'd be coming home one of these days. I can't endure it by myself much longer."

Now all the responsibilities are on him—to keep up the home and Jeep. At the thought of Jeep, Chris feels a twinge of guilt. Despite his best intentions, Chris knows he isn't doing a very good job as a father. More often than not, it was Jeep taking care of him, by doing the cooking and chores.

I'll have to talk with him about her one of these days, he decides, as he'd often done before. Then he never got around to it. *Better he doesn't know, better that he has hope to hang on to—I sure wish I did.*

Chris writes the checks and inserts them into the preprinted envelopes. Such a routine activity, yet each month it's more distressing. It makes him feel as inadequate as his bank balance.

Chris dozes off midway through and is awakened in the morning by Jeep, who is still in his pajamas.

"Hey, didn't you ever get to bed?"

"Huh?" Chris asks, still half asleep. He stumbles toward the bathroom.

Jeep follows him, "You OK? You look awful. Want me to call you in sick?"

"I'm OK. Maybe a shower…" He closes the door so he won't have to look at Jeep's worried face.

But Jeep isn't fooled. He realizes that Chris is struggling to act normal.

CHAPTER 9
THE RETURN TO
GRIKKL'S WORLD

The following Saturday morning Chris says to Jeep, "Let's have breakfast at Mildred's Place. You and I probably should talk."

Jeep is relieved since they hardly exchanged a word since their clash. Tension between them still hangs in the air.

Mildred's Place is their favorite café. If there ever had been a Mildred, she is long gone. Their waitress is Phyllis, who has served them as long as they've eaten at Mildred's.

When they arrive, the dining room is already about two-thirds full, and filling up fast.

Chris gets a mug of coffee, then gives Phyllis his order—sausage, French toast, and two eggs, over-easy. Jeep never looks at the menu since he always gets the same thing—hash browns, scrambled eggs, bacon, and a crispy English muffin.

While they waited for their food, Chris speaks. "I've been thinking about what you said, Jeep. It makes sense you want to see your mom. I wanted to protect you, that's all. But I reckon you're old enough to know the truth."

"So, I get to see her? You'll take me?" Jeep is almost afraid to hope.

"Sure, the next Wednesday I go, you can come. But I still think it's not a good idea. Like I said, she's not just sick—it's mental. Maybe you'll stop blaming me…"

Jeep isn't listening to the rest. He's way too excited. *At last I'm going to see Mom!*

About then, Phyllis arrives with their food. They are used to her being efficient, and quick with a clever remark. Today she isn't like her ordinary self. She seems to be off-balance. Sunny-side-up eggs arrive instead of eggs over-easy. And she forgot Chris's syrup.

Jeep doesn't fare any better—his English muffin is barely toasted and is already cold (horrors!). Chris and Jeep point out the mistakes and Phyllis takes their food away to correct the order.

Jeep and Chris are in for a ridiculously long wait before they'd see their food again. Phyllis' section is full, and all the customers expect service at the same time. The ever-cheerful Phyllis is stressed out and error-prone.

Jeep notices her struggling to keep up—even poorly. *Here I am feeling so happy but Phyllis needs a lift, too.*

Jeep whispers to Chris, "Let's raise her spirits. I'm going to make Phyllis think we're the best customers she's ever had.

Her next trip past their table Jeep chants, "You're doing great! Go! Go! Go!" like he's her cheerleader. She looked so rattled he can't tell if she heard. Jeep kept making goofy faces at her and sending her the "thumbs up" signal each time she hurries by. Chris plays along.

When their correct order finally arrives, Jeep tells her, "Phyllis, we like to eat here because of you. You're the best thing on the menu. I'll bet all these people agree. This bunch of people is your fan club. They all showed up today *for you*."

A wisp of a smile appears on her lips. Gradually, her fogginess thins. When she makes a witty remark to them, there she is! The Phyllis who Chris and Jeep like so much is back.

Their efforts to cheer Phyllis up are rather pleasant for themselves as well. Chris tells about a British customer who expected free delivery of a bed—all the way to England. For his part, Jeep repeats descriptions of what Cindy told him about the strange foods she ate in Korea.

Before long, the two of them are laughing like long-time friends. They hadn't acted that friendly with each other, even when Helen was home. That morning some long-standing discomfort between them leaked away. Chris begins to realize he can be a good father, without being stern and distant, like his own father had been.

Jeep is ready the next time Merve's crew picks on them. He yells, "Hey, you apes! Cut that out!" They notice him as little as a thick-skinned elephant worries about a mosquito.

Jeep tugs hard on Merve's sleeve and hollers, "Leave them alone! You jerks can't treat people like that."

Merve shrugs him off. "It's none of your business, Jeep the Creep."

Totally ignored—how humiliating! Hurts worse than a bloody nose would. Embarrassed, frustrated, yet determined to sidetrack the tormentors, Jeep lobs a half-inch rock at Merve.

Ping. Direct hit—right on his chin. Although it isn't very hard, that certainly gets Merve's attention. Merve spins away from Anna, then charges after Jeep like an angry rhino. His buddies chase behind.

Jeep bolts, dodging around parked cars. *If they catch me, they'll get me good.* Although he is still ahead, he isn't a good runner. Jeep realizes he can't last much longer. *Why? Why was I so stupid?*

Merve and his crew are getting closer. Jeep hears the flap-flapping of their tennis shoes as they gain on him.

Any moment they'll catch me. I don't stand a chance. Jeep gasps, fighting for air. Unable to catch his breath, he presses both hands against his chest. His fingers accidentally brush his rabbit medallion, and his thoughts go to Lulu.

A zizz of happy memories waft over him. As his hands clutch the medallion the magic happens.

(Blip)

Jeep appears abruptly in Grikkl's cozy living space. His panting body plops out of the air and bounces heavily onto the sofa by the fireplace.

"I'm safe…! I'm safe…!" is all the surprised and breathless Jeep can gasp—or grasp. He shakes with relief, overcome with gratitude and wonder for his unlikely escape.

Lulu hops over to him and rubs against his leg, as if he has never been gone. Adah rushes to his side and engulfs him in her welcoming arms.

"Jeep, you're back so soon!"

"I suppose… How'd I get here?"

"Binkle power. I knew you had a knack. You're like a little bird that leaves the nest and manages to find its own worms."

"I hope you're talking about binkles, not worms. But I knew I had to find enough binkles every day on my own so I could get back here."

"It must have worked 'cuz here you are!"

"You'll give me plenty of them while I'm here, won't you?" Adah cradles him tighter in her arms.

"Don't you know that whenever you give a binkle you get one? They're about sharing! I get fed inside as much as you do every time you and I connect."

She lets go of him but holds his gaze for a long moment. "My dear Jeep, I'm so glad you're back. Grikkl's grown tired of my songs and I know all of his stories. You…" She beams even brighter at him. "You *want* to hear me sing, and keep asking for more. How can I thank you?"

"Thank me? It's me who should be thanking you. What you give me is much more than songs and stories. You make me happy."

Adah tussles his hair in reply. She sings him the Bee Song— another favorite song about flying, only not so high.

As she sings, he feels himself tirelessly flying from flower to flower. He senses himself float slowly over flower beds, pausing to burrow his face into blossom after blossom, as he breathes in their many-flavored scents.

When he finally returns to the hive, other bees gather around to taste the pollen clinging to him, so they could enjoy the same flavors. Jeep the Bee wiggles an intricate dance for the other bees that tells them where to find the flowers with the pollen they just tasted on him.

Through Adah's song, Jeep experiences a bee's life as a diligent search for blossoms. As such, he enjoys riding the shifting breezes and feeling the warm sun or cool shadows as he goes about his never-ending work. *Ah, the life of a bee, I like that.*

Grikkl ambles over to them once Adah finishes her singing. "Now tell, Laddie. We want to hear about what you learned out there on your own."

The three of them again sit in front of the fireplace, but this time Jeep does most of the talking. He tells them about the little ways his life at home and school changed after he went back—more energy, more variety in how he spends his time.

The old couple chuckles when Jeep describes spending so much time with the very same people he used to avoid. Adah praises his spunk and willingness to try to things he didn't like—just in the hope of a binkle. But hearing Jeep's joy in having a marvelous secret is the part the gnomes like best.

As they talk further about binkle power, Adah says, "Life is sprinkled with perfect moments, kind of like pepper. Whenever you binkle, you're spreading more of that pepper around. You cannot avoid getting some on yourself whenever you sprinkle it on others. And by binkling that makes more good feelings for everyone."

Lulu sticks to Jeep as if she's glued to him, but he spends time every day with Cerberus as well. Jeep asks the dog, "Don't you ever leave?"

"Sure, but I'm so fast that no one ever sees me coming and going. I'm gone and back in a flash. Walls present no barrier to me. Besides, most of my trips take me to other dimensions, or Fairyland, where the fairy folk live. Over there, they treat me like the mailman."

"But I thought things like that get done by magic."

"That's only halfway true. But magic or not, the mail gets through because *I deliver it.* You know the saying, 'Neither rain, nor snow, nor sleet, nor dark of night…'? That's about me. See my mailbags?"

The dog gestures toward the gear on his back.

"I was meaning to ask you about what it's for. I thought it was a saddle."

"That's a good one, Jeep. Who do you think would ride me?"

"Grikkl?

Cerberus bursts out laughing with a wheezy, yodeling sound. He laughs harder and harder, louder and louder, more like yodeling all the time. The dog is so consumed by laughter he falls over. His right front paw waives in the air, as he pounds the floor with his left one. More than once, his riotous laughter peters out, only to start up all over again.

"I don't think it's that funny" said Jeep. Maybe it was a dumb thing to say, but don't make fun of me. I didn't know."

Cerberus is wheezing too hard to answer. Feeling put down and embarrassed, Jeep moves away to be by himself. *I've been made fun of too many times, but didn't expect that here. And not from a dog.*

Jeep tries to ignore Cerberus' chuckles and floor pounding without success. But soon Lulu leaps into his lap and her boundless affection makes him forget.

From then on, Cerberus treats Jeep as good for a laugh. The dog would ask him a riddle or tell a joke with Jeep as his straight man. Although Jeep's ability to understand the dog's words improved, he never got the point of the dog's jokes.

They depended on experiences he, as a human, didn't have. Like when Cerberus asks, "How is a fairy like a hummingbird?" the answer (taller than a finger) doesn't make sense to him. Even when I'm told the answer it doesn't seem funny.

Jeep's bewilderment just makes Cerberus laugh at him all over again. "Is the real joke on me?" Jeep asks the dog, which just brings on more chuckles.

Jeep decides to tell Cerberus a few jokes he knows about cannibals.

"What did the mother cannibal say to her child? (Pause) 'Eat your soup before it clots.'

"Two cannibals ate a clown. Later, one cannibal asks the other one, 'Did that taste funny to you?'"

Cerberus doesn't get Jeep's jokes either, but replies, "Bad jokes! Cannibals aren't funny. Now elves, they're funny. Or wizards, they're really funny. But cannibals aren't funny at all." Then the dog snickers smugly at his own wittiness.

One day Jeep asks Adah about something that's bothering him. "You and Grikkl said that sending me home was a test, to see if I could find enough binkle power without any help. I got enough to get back here. Since I passed the test, can't I stay here now?"

Adah replies in a way that is both kindly and stern. "There's still very much for you to learn. You must be able to live in your own world and play by those rules too. This isn't a place to escape from life's challenges."

"But I'm safe with you. Nothing scares me here."

"Learning to master your fears is one of those difficult lessons. I would be doing you no favors if I tried to make your path easy for you. Indeed, super-human strength and character are required for certain portions of the journey.

"And you can't accomplish that unless you know how to get past your fears. The scary parts won't go away, but you'll know you can handle them."

Grikkl also talks to Jeep in more detail about being afraid. "Fear can be a good thing or bad thing, depending on what you do about it. It can shut down your brain for the moment or even a long time. That's natural. We're all afraid once in a while.

"But think of fear as just a warning—Be careful! So, pay even more attention—don't ignore those messages or give in to them. There are always more choices than the obvious ones. See if you can notice your fear—without it scaring you. Besides, you could never know courage if it weren't for fear."

Jeep grabs his head as though it's about to explode. "That doesn't make sense. Fear, scared, afraid—they sound like the same thing to me."

"But they're not the same at all! Fear doesn't do you harm— unless you let it scare you."

"Are you telling me it's OK to be afraid? I should like it? I don't like the sound of that."

"Fear is no fun, I'll grant you. But notice where the fear is coming from. Is it from something that's actually dangerous? Or is it coming from your thoughts getting all worked up about it?

"Don't get fooled because something is frightening. That doesn't mean you have to be scared by it. With a cool head, you can deal with what's the problem. But fear that scrambles your thinking and makes you doubt yourself. Well, that's never going to resolve anything."

Jeep shakes his head, as though this jumble of conflicting ideas could settle into a place that makes sense. "So, what should I do instead?"

"I've got two answers. First say 'Boo!' Let the scary thoughts know you're able to see right through them. They're no more real than ghosts to you."

Jeep said, "I suppose the other is about binkles…"

Adah laughs. "Oh Jeep, you know me so well; but you're right. Treat whatever you're afraid of like a sign that flashes, 'Find a binkle here.' By the time you figure out how to get a binkle in that less-than-pleasant situation you've forgotten to be scared. And binkle or not, you've gotten something even better besides—those fears didn't get you."

"Adah, even if you're right, I've been scared way too often to take a chance. It doesn't work that way for me. If I see a sign it would say, 'Stay away!' Do you really think a few binkles can make me brave?" Jeep makes an exaggerated face that clearly communicates he doesn't think so.

Grikkl said, "There's a story… Let me tell you about a young African girl who overcame her fears. Her name was Mella. Her father was very ill. and the medicines couldn't cure him. She fears he will die, so she asks the moon goddess what to do. The goddess tells her to get help from the Python Healer.

"That advice scares Mella since even the bravest men in the village are too frightened to speak after going to his cave. But she loves her father so much that she puts her fears aside and walks four days to the Python Healer's cave.

"The snake tells her, 'You're a foolish girl who should be afraid of me, like all of the other people from your village.'

"She answers, 'I do fear you. But my love for my father speaks louder to me than my fears do.'

"The python asks her, 'If your love is more powerful than your fear of me, will you let me wind myself around your body? (A python kills its victim by coiling around it and crushing the body to death; then it swallows the body whole.)

"Mella hesitates, but only for a moment. By letting the snake wrap himself around her, she proves she is more courageous than the brave men who ran from it. Mella carries the snake for four days, as they go back to her father. When they arrive, the snake is able to cure him. Her father is very grateful and praises both Mella and the snake. Then Mella carries the snake coiled around herself another four days, all the way back to his cave.

"At the snake's cave, the Python Healer says to her, 'Mella, you are both wise and brave. You've learned that courage and love are stronger than fear.'"

Grikkl ends, "Jeep, I hope this myth helps you see what's possible when a person has enough courage to face their fears. Mella was even strong enough to build trust with a snake. It's not a bad thing to have fears—if you can do what you know is right, anyway."

CHAPTER 10
THE FACE OF EVIL

Another time, Adah tells Jeep, "Don't be afraid of your emotions. Fear is just one of them. They're your heart entering into the conversation. Into the experience. Emotions add the color, the sparkle to life."

"But my emotions are so rotten, I don't want to feel them. Better that I push them away."

"My dear boy. If you shut off your emotions, you shut them *all* off. Not just the yucky ones. You turn off the love and joy too. You've got a lot to learn about riding the emotional roller coaster. Life is not all ups—it can't be."

"But the downs don't feel good. Better to shut them out," Jeep insists.

"Don't act surprised when I tell you the way out of ups and downs is binkles. They can turn a down into an up—or an up into a way-up. There are no yucky binkles. When your heart is happy, you forget about being miserable, or angry, or even annoyed. So, the downs won't pull you down with it."

"Of course, your answer to everything. More binkles," scoffs Jeep.

"And why not, pray tell?" asks Adah with a waving finger. "Since it is."

"I'll not argue with you—for a hug. I think I'm catching on how this works," he winks.

A day later Grikkl asks, "Want to go back to the Chamber of Ancient Wisdom?"

"You bet! Been hoping you'd ask. Only this time I'm going to explore in one place instead of leapfrogging all over."

"Suit yourself. Lots of remarkable stuff there. Too much for the mind to entertain. Even I'm overwhelmed by wonder at all that's in there.

As before, Cerberus leads the way until they reached the rock walls blocking the tunnel. Grikkl chants at the first obstruction. At the next he blows the musical notes to move the rock wall aside.

When they reach the two identical wooden doors, Cerberus takes charge. He sniffs, makes low woofing sounds, and listens. Finally, the dog lies down in front of the door to the right. Today, at least, that door is the safe one.

But Jeep is badly shaken by the dog's choice. While Cerberus goes through his routine, Jeep decided which door he'd choose if it were up to him. *I chose is the wrong door! (Fortunately, only taken in my mind.) Without Cerberus I'd have taken The Door of No Return.*

Grikkl notices Jeep's distress and clamps him on the shoulder. "By now you should be knowing that this is a serious business.

The fight against evil is not all rainbows and happy thoughts. Binkles are powerful, but they must be protected."

"But surely we're safe here? Jeep asks somewhere between an assertion and a question in his voice.

"I wish that were true, Laddie. But you must never underestimate your opponent. And the 'Stamp out the Binkle team' will stop at nothing. These protections are not just for show."

Once inside the Chamber, Grikkl leads Jeep to a nook hung with works of art. Several elaborate tapestries displayed on the rock wall show a unicorn.

"Take a look at these, Laddie. You've probably seen unicorn pictures like them.

"Sure, I've seen unicorns before," Jeep answers without much interest. "Are they real? To listen to Adah, you'd think so."

"Adah has known a few unicorns in her time, that's true. The better question is whether or not they're real *for you*."

"It's just a horse with a horn."

"Not so, Laddie—not even close. Would it surprise you to know those legends about unicorns are actually tales about the power of binkles?"

"How's that?"

"Glad you asked. That's what we're here to talk about. It's a fearsome power that binkles and unicorns represent. And tales about them do not always have a happy ending."

Grikkl gestures around the enormous, packed cavern. "Just being here needs to be a reminder to you that the mythic battles between light and dark involved real people, real suffering. They were BATTLES. Two sides fighting to the death if necessary. And the unicorn is a fitting symbol for it."

The gnome and boy settle into their seats, with Grikkl propping his feet on a nearby trunk. Grikkl's tone and manner that day sound like a history lesson.

"The unicorn has appeared in folklore for thousands of years. It's a symbol of supreme power, a power that's sought by all. Those ancient tales are as dissimilar as the minds that wrote them. But as much as those tales differ, they all agree that the unicorn is powerful.

"The creatures were a common symbol during the Middle Ages, when those tapestries over there were made. To be precise, the unicorn represents a blend of power and purity.

And because of that, it is always in danger. Kings and soldiers tried to capture it in order to possess its remarkable strength.

"They didn't understand that the unicorn can't be controlled, not by weapons anyway. Its immense power cannot be taken by force. It can only be shared willingly. They didn't realize where a unicorn's power comes from. Why it works. So even if they can capture or kill that noble creature they still can't gain the true source of its power.

"But wasn't that a long time ago?"

"True enough, Laddie. Even so, the unicorn matters to you today. It stands for binkle power as a living, potent force in the world. The maiden represents innocence and purity of spirit. She loves the unicorn. It loves her back—heart to heart. They make binkles together.

"Both of them are pure in heart. Together, they create a living force, a force for good. And just like it was back then, even today that power is still in peril. Binkle power is vulnerable, not because it is weak, but because those who love power for themselves want to control it. Evil cannot create binkle energy, so they try to take it away from those who can.

"Adah and I, and unnamed others, are devoted to protecting the binkle. I'm sad to say the days are dark, and evil forces once again threaten the world. A major conflict is near at hand. Many signs indicate that the evil ones are gaining strength.

"Ancient people understood this wisdom about binkle power. But most of what was widely known has been lost except to those few who passed it on one person at a time. Like I'm doing now with you.

"The loss was sometimes accidental, but more often than not it happened because evil forces wanted it that way. There have always been wicked people whose power depends on this wisdom remaining forgotten.

"Binkle power promotes goodness and provides protection against wickedness. When a person acquires enough of its special energy, it becomes impossible for them to be fooled by lies or liars, in any of their many forms."

Grikkl's tone shifts from being a lecture to sounding quite grim. "So far, Jeep, you've been getting to know the gentler side of binkles. The fun of it. But there's a darker side, too. Those who want to control binkle energy are ruthless. If they can't control it, they're just as willing to destroy it—like they've done with the unicorn."

"But why? Who wouldn't want binkles? They make me happy. They make everybody happy, don't they?"

"Yes, happiness… who wouldn't want that? Believe me, there are plenty of people who get their pleasure from taking other people's joy away. It's a dark kind of power that doesn't want joyful energy around.

"When a person gets enough binkle energy regularly they have more confidence. People without joy and energy are much easier to control. So, if someone wanted to control them, an easy way is to crush their spirits, make them weak. Now, can't you see why wicked men want this knowledge to stay forgotten?"

As Grikkl speaks, his manner becomes increasingly agitated. Jeep has never seen Grikkl in such a frantic state before. His words trail off, his mind far away, as Grikkl idly rubs his foot.

The silence is broken by a tormented cry, which almost makes Jeep jump out of his skin.

"Uuglash! You must learn to recognize and fear Uuglash," Grikkl snarls. "He's pure evil—the face of your enemy and mine. He's the killer of hope and joy, the destroyer of innocence and integrity. It's dark evil, for the pleasure it gives him.

"Even his name is unsavory—so nasty you want to spit it out. It's old, older than any language you'd recognize—sounding like grunting. There's no civilized name for him. But I'll bet you've never even heard about him, have you?"

Jeep shakes his head, frightened by Grikkl's angry outburst. "No, not unless he uses other names…"

"Disguises, you mean. That he does. Lots of them. He keeps popping up in one form or another all through history. Bad things happen whenever he shows up—really bad. But if you look beneath the surface you'll find Uuglash, alright—a force for pure hate. Power gone mad—that's him.

"You don't encounter Uuglash face to face often—he's too smart for that. He has helpers—legions of them. He infects the minds of power-hungry thugs who are eager to do his bidding. It's their foul names that history records. They take the credit as though their malice is something to be proud of. But behind them you'll find Uuglash—if you know what to look for."

Each time Grikkl says "Uuglash" he snarls. And his anger goes up another notch. "He's real! Not just an old gnome ranting on. Not by a long shot. I can prove it, just so you know."

Grikkl's feet still rest on the crate. He leans forward and ever so slowly removes his left boot—suspense building all the while. Jeep bends over to better see what Grikkl is doing.

When his sock comes off, there it is—impossible to miss! Jeep gasps and looks away, both horrified and sickened by the awful evidence.

Half his left foot and all its toes and are gone!

"Does it hurt?" Jeep can't help asking.

"The pain's still there, Laddie, but it's in my head—every time I think about him. Every time I see Uuglash's mark on me. It was horrible—still is. Though it happened a hundred years ago. Whenever I look at my poor excuse for a foot it stings like a searing fire all over again. It feels like it's a fresh, bleeding wound."

"How did it happen?"

"Just a moment's inattention… I was lucky to escape at all."

Grikkl grimaces as he relives the horrible encounter in his memory. He sits in silence for several minutes.

By the time Grikkl speaks again, his mood has brightened a bit. While not yet his usual buoyant self, his dark mood is receding.

"Hey, maybe I'm like Captain Hook—forever in pursuit of the one who lopped off my limb. Neither one of us can have peace while the other lives."

"But how…," Jeep tries to ask again.

"Not now, Laddie. Not here." Grikkl glances slowly about the Chamber, a tangible monument to the binkle's might against the foes of goodness.

"Let's stop a while. Poke around in the loot around here. Bound to be more entertaining than listening to me reliving ancient history."

As much as Jeep wants to look around, it doesn't feel right to leave Grikkl by himself just then.

"Another time. Better I sit here with you."

"That's alright, Laddie. I'll be back to myself in a few minutes. Don't worry about 'ole Grikkl. I've lived with this injury a long time. Go on. I need to be by myself."

Jeep heads straight to an enormous pile that looks like loot from sunken treasure-laden ships. The hoard must have been underwater a long time because barnacles and crusted deposits once covered much of it. The heavy wooden chests overflow with gold. Some is in bars or coins, but even more of it is cast into delicate jewelry and statues that were cast in olden times. Jeep asks if it's pirate treasure.

"Aye, Laddie, pirates stole it but they didn't get to keep it." Grikkl describes fearsome sea battles in which the pirates were defeated. "Brave captains turned the tide against those vicious, blood-thirsty beasts who preyed on sailing ships. Many ships were sunk on both sides—so much life lost. The treasure in front of you is all that's left.

"Those perilous times make for a distressing tale, though one overflowing with bravery and honor. What you're digging through is more than a king's ransom, for sure.

 "But if their ships were lost, how did their treasure end up here? Who lived to tell about it?"

"Why, it was the mermaids and mermen themselves who saw it all. The People of the Deep passed the word to those they trusted. Otherwise, no human would ever have learned what happened. Dangerous battles spread over years. Wreckage of it is far apart, littered across the ocean floor.

"Now, I'm not one to criticize, but usually you can't expect much from mermaids when there's work to be done. They're happy just to drift along on the sea currents and sing their wattery songs. But they offered to bring up this whole lot. And they made a real job of it, too. You can thank the mermaids for rescuing the treasure you see there—a worthy reminder of those long-dead heroes."

Once seated again, Grikkl leans forward and speaks just above a whisper, like he's confiding a secret. *Can't imagine what could be even more mysterious or important than what he's already told me.*

"Binkle energy is so important for our survival that everyone has an organ inside of us to monitor how much of that energy a body has. It's called the krindle."

"Never heard of it."

"Of course not. Its very existence is part of the lost wisdom."

"But Grikkl, how can the human body have an organ that science hasn't discovered?"

"The organ is known to exist, sure enough. It's right there in the anatomy books, though with different names than 'krindle.' But it's not just the work of a single organ. Some of its functions are performed by the pineal gland in the middle of the brain; some functions take place in the heart.

"They connect you up to higher-vibration energy. But scientists didn't have a clue about these purposes. And like most important secrets, it's all hidden in plain sight—nice as you please. A person has to know what to look for in order to recognize the krindle's vital function.

"Science doesn't know about binkle energy or how badly people rely on it for their health and happiness. Too bad, since binkle power acts as a curative tonic. It resonates with enough high-octane energy to recharge the mind, flesh, and emotions—all at the same time. It keeps them all healthy. "Everybody needs binkles every day—they're stronger than vitamins for making the body and mind work the way they're supposed to. When a person can't get enough binkles, their krindle starts to dry up. If they go too long without them, the krindle could be destroyed... forever."

Jeep gasps, "You mean, there won't be any more binkles for them?"

"Aye. Laddie. It feels almost as bad as a death sentence. They're condemned to a flat and joyless existence."

Jeep shudders. Grikkl pats his shoulder until the horror of what that would mean for somebody fades.

When Grikkl resumes, he asks, "Remember when I told you that you'll need to learn to protect yourself? It's Uuglash and his lot you'll need protection from."

"Why would they care about me? I'm a kid. I can't do anything to them."

Grikkl pauses as he fiddles with his beard. "Maybe not yet, but one day you could be a threat to them. Sooner or later, they're bound to detect what you're up to. You'll leave a trail of happier people, and they'll notice you.

"Those nasty characters are smart enough to take you down before you understand how to use so much power. It might not happen right away—but it could. They might come after you when you least expect it. So, you'd have to defend yourself. That's one possibility."

Grikkl's voice drops ominously. His eyes pierce into Jeep's. "But there's another possibility that worries me more, Jeep. You could invite them in. Invite them in…"

"I'd never do that, Grikkl. I don't want anything to do with them."

"I know that, Jeep. That's not what's worrying me. Remember, they're the bad ones—they like to do terrible things to other people. The world of evil is where they live and play. Being wicked just makes them stronger, more evil.

"You're not like that—not at all. You couldn't ever be as good at being bad as they are, understand?" He waits until Jeep nods that he is following.

"The main way a person invites them in is to forget to trust the power of goodness. Instead, the person relies on evil methods to get something that they want. That's *their* game, remember?"

BANG! An explosive crash echoes through the cavern. The sound startles Jeep so much he jumps as if he's been shot.

The loud noise came from Grikkl slamming two heavy books together. Then he repeats the sound by voice.

"Bang! Just like that... Bang! They've got you! You're theirs—because you invited them in."

A shaken Jeep asks, "What if I didn't mean to? Can't I get rid of them?"

"Sure, you can push them out. Anyone can slip up once in a while, but these evil ones are like termites. If you keep letting them in they just get harder to get rid of the next time. One day, you let them stay without minding too much, and they've got you!

"The reason why that risk is worse for you than for most people is you're getting stronger in ways that matter. Your krindle works better. And it's going to get stronger yet.

"If you let evil come in to stay, your krindle could stop working at all. It needs considerable binkle energy to make it strong, to keep it functioning. If you're doing bad things, that's the same as krindle poisoning.

"Uuglash's team wins both ways—whether they hurt you bad enough to make you stop, or whether you shut down your krindle through your own negative behavior. Can't you see why you'd be a real prize for them?"

Again, Grikkl nods gravely and holds Jeep's gaze for a long moment.

"Not to mention the fact they'd like nothing better than to hurt one of my apprentices. They'd welcome a chance to take a poke at me, too."

Jeep voice quivers. "Now…, now…, now hold on a second, Grikkl. Did I just hear you say you consider me your apprentice?"

"Aye, Laddie. It is true."

"That's news to me. Does that mean you'll be teaching me what you know?"

"Aye, a chunk of it anyway. We'll get to that in good time…

"Just so you know, I officially accept," Jeep announces with a big grin on his face. "I'm your apprentice."

"Before you get all excited about that, there's a serious matter for you and me to work out."

"Whatever you say."

"Remember when you threw the rock at Merve? When you used force against him that way, you weren't any better than he was.

"Throwing the rock or trying to hurt somebody is exactly the kind of behavior that invites Uuglash in. No real harm done yet, but be forewarned. It matters."

"But I was scared."

"Aye, fear calls them, like bees to a blossom. But yielding to fear makes you weaker and their side stronger. Even if you're frightened, you must *never be mean*—NO MATTER WHAT."

"OK. I get it. I believe you. I'll be careful."

"It's much more dangerous to you than you realize. Promise me that you won't allow yourself to act without honor."

Jeep puts his hand over his heart and solemnly pledges, "With all the power that's in me, I promise. I'll never be mean again, Grikkl. Never."

"Aye, I know you'll do your best."

Grikkl pats Jeep's shoulder. "But one last word. What I've been telling isn't just about you, you know. There's a war—it's been going on for a really long time.

"People lined up on the side of light must fight against the evils of the dark side. Both sides have their famed warriors and their preferred ways of working.

"We're the good guy team—don't you ever forget it, Jeep. When you're strong, you help our team. When you're weak...." He lets the unspoken words hang like a threat in the air. Jeep still got it.

Talk shifts to other, less dire matters. Too soon, it's time to go. Like his prior trip, Jeep's mind is spinning as he tries to make sense of all he was told that day. And he makes the return trip in a daze.

CHAPTER 11
SEALING THE RIFT

Adah takes every chance she gets to hug Jeep and beam affectionately at him. She likes to do it—but no more than he likes her to. *Silly idea, as if you could ever tell who likes hugging the most.*

She once told him, "I've done so many amazing things in my long lifetime you'd suspect I have eerie powers. Nothing major, like a super-power. But they add up, so in the end the problem gets resolved.

"Some who know me call me 'A Priestess of Another Sort.' I do work a bit of magic into what I do. But my favorite trick is making a sad boy smile."

Jeep grins, "It must be working, since I smile most of the time I'm around you."

"That's good—but just the start. It's easy around me. You need to find moments like this anywhere you find yourself. Or with anyone you meet. That's how *you make magic* too.

"A binkle feeling doesn't just depend on words or what people say to you. Sometimes, you'll feel binkles bubbling up from a joyful thought, or a favorite song, or a dazzling sunset, or a soft, cuddly kitten, or just because you did something nice.

"Once you're looking for them, they can come from anyone or anywhere. Finding them makes your life sparkle."

"I know! I never knew so many things could feel good. Does it work like that for everyone?"

"Could be—it's up to them. That feeling certainly makes a body glad to be alive, doesn't it? High-binkle experiences are at the heart of our favorite memories. I'm sure some stand out for you—especially some things you did with your mother."

"I remember when Mom and I got MeToo. That was great!"

"Tell me. I want to hear the details, so I can see what happened along with you."

"We saw a little girl with a box of puppies in a parking lot. I wanted a dog for a long time. But that was the first time we lived in a place with a yard. There were five wiggly, soft and smooshy bodies bumped together—all with big eyes and floppy ears. All watchful of me as I reached out to pat them.

"Mom told me I could take one home—Oh happy day! But which? Not an easy choice when there's so much cuteness, so many almost-alike bundles of furry affection. She told me not to rush, but already other people were taking an interest. So, if I didn't hurry there'd be fewer to choose from.

"I picked up the closest one and held it against my cheek. Heaven! Then I picked up another, then another. Each one, heaven. By then I wasn't sure which of the puppies I missed.

And I still didn't know how to choose. I loved them all too much to pick just one.

"It turned out the choice was made *for* me. One little puppy climbed over his littermates and tried to climb my leg. He was so endearing, the rest didn't have a chance. So that's how I got him."

"Then MeToo picked you. Like Lulu. The hearts did the picking."

Jeep also tells about the time he and MeToo rolled in the grass together until he was so happy all over he wanted to be a dog himself.

"Oh Jeep, I got a zizz just from you sharing your special memories. Bet you did too."

"I guess, but it doesn't happen to feel good every time. Sometimes remembering the good times makes me sad instead. I miss them so much, and feel times like that are gone for good."

"True, memories can pull you up or bring you down. But it's always worth a try to revisit the high-binkle ones. Even trying will change the way you act around other people— making them warm up to you.

"Sometimes it's easier to form friendships with animals."

Adah calls toward the raven perched as usual hear the top of the fireplace, "Ramses, come over here. I don't think you and Jeep have gotten to know each other proper."

Ramses drifts slowly down and lands on the tall back of a chair that put him eye-to-eye with Jeep. The bird says, "I've noticed how much you like Adah's flying song."

"Sure, it's my favorite."

The bird and boy are soon chattering on like old buddies. Jeep loves being told little-known details about bird life. Like how to find the fattest worms, or what a caterpillar tastes like. And how they know when it's time to leave the nest and mama bird.

Adah says, "Ramses has a distinguished heritage. Ravens are a well-known symbol of ancient wisdom and magic."

Ramses stands up proudly as Adah describes the noble achievements of his distant ancestors.

"American Indians always treated the raven as sacred. They consider Raven heroic—fighting to right wrongs and punish evil doers. According to Indian lore, Raven existed even before creation and helped to make the world. That's probably a stretch, but ravens deserve respect, don't they, Ramses?"

While Adah is describing his ancestry, Ramses shifts from looking regal to seeming downright annoyed.

Jeep asks, "What's the matter, Ramses?"

The bird is glad to have someone new to complain to. It launches into an oft-repeated grievance.

"You heard what Adah said. My ancestors were important—and powerful. Ravens were respected in Egypt and among the Indian tribes. They were treated as wise and brave—our feats the stuff of legends. And all of that, all that achievement was wrecked by one man."

As he warms to his subject, Ramses' voice becomes more shrill and irritated. "It's not fair, I tell you. Not fair! Our greatness, all that my kind achieved, is forgotten just because of one stupid poem.[2]"

Jeep said, "I'm not following you." But it's clear that Adah has heard it all before, because she excuses herself and hurries away.

"There was this guy named Poe who lived a long time ago, see. Anyway, he probably was an OK writer. But he wrote this poem, see? And this raven in the poem said just one word over and over all through the poem—'nevermore.'

"And this poem got real famous. So, for 150 years people have heard the raven with just one word to say. 'Nevermore,'—just 'nevermore,' over and over again. Now I ask you, isn't that a pretty dumb bird?"

---

[2] The Raven," by Edgar Allen Poe. © 1845

Ramses paces back and forth along the back of the chair, shaking his head in outrage at the injustice of it all.

"'Nevermore,' Is that any way to talk? That man just made all of us ravens look dumb. We're not, you know. But because of that poem we sure sound stupid."

"I don't see what's so bad about…"

"You don't do you! What do you know, anyway? If you say 'raven' to just about anybody, what do they say back to you? I'll tell you what. They'll nod and say, like they're being clever, 'Nevermore.' People don't remember any of our good stuff—just that dumb bird from Poe."

Jeep says something sympathetic, but that isn't what Ramses wants to hear. The irate bird just wants to complain about the unfairness of it all.

"I don't intend to let that poem be the last word on ravens, see. Here's my real last word on it. Nevermore will I say 'nevermore!' It's gone, kaput! Out of my vocabulary for good. You won't ever hear me say 'nevermore' again."

By the time Ramses stops talking, Jeep sincerely hopes that is true.

The next day, Grikkl says, "I filled your head with more than anyone can swallow in one gulp. Though everything I've told you is true, it doesn't become true for you until you can put it to use. Put it into your life.

"Today your brain needs a rest and I need help outdoors. Magic or not, plenty of what needs doing around here boils down to hard work. Want to help?"

"Sure, I'm game. I could use some fresh air, and maybe even some daylight."

They dress warm to protect from the crisp wind of winter. Grikkl carries a mysterious-shaped package. He hands Jeep a pair of ice-skate-like contraptions to lug along. The pair move in silence until they reach the edge of the woods.

Grikkl instructs Jeep, "Put those thinger-dingers on over your shoes."

Once Jeep fastens them on, his feet are about five inches above the ground. He rocks from side to side on his strange footgear, as he gets used to the unnatural way they made him move. At first, they feel awkward. But with only a little practice he can keep his balance without wobbling.

The thinger-dingers cleverly hide his tracks. Instead of making a trail of his own footprints, he now leaves a trail of raccoon paw prints. If someone had bothered to follow the tracks Jeep made that day, they'd think they stumbled upon the trail of a dancing and leaping raccoon.

Grikkl explains what needs to be done. "The repairs we're making must be done in such a way that no one can tell that anybody has been here. My way of walking doesn't leave footprints. And your leaving raccoon tracks allows us to move freely.

"I need to fix a tear in the protective shield that keeps this place invisible to outsiders." *That explains how there could be a magic wood so close to town. That's why I only got here by falling down the cliff.*

"If this gap isn't repaired strangers might accidentally wander in. The greater danger though, would be that Uuglash's followers could find us. The intense, concentrated energy leaking out would surely get their attention soon enough."

Jeep has to follow Grikkl's instructions to the last detail since he is unable to see the rift that is being fixed. They use a nearly invisible cord as lightweight as cobwebs, while being incredibly strong.

All afternoon Jeep measures, cuts, ties, tacks, and loops invisible stuff together wherever Grikkl directs him to do so. More than once he accidentally drops a piece of the gossamer cord and has a tough time finding it or picking it up with his fingers.

As each section of the tear is securely tightened, Grikkl performs the same baffling ceremony. He rings a silver bell as he chants in slow, deep, resonant tones ("nom pon deedee da, pause, looda sham"). After that, he throws a pinch of sparkly orange powder from a small leather bag against the area just repaired.

The orange sparkles are the only sign of the repaired fabric that Jeep can actually see. And even those spots soon fade away.

After that, Grikkl would swing the device (which was in the odd-shaped package) around his head six times as he repeats the chant ("nom pon deedee da, pause, looda sham").

Jeep asks, "What does that gadget do?"

Grikkl puts his finger to his lips, shakes his head and blows, "Shhh…"

As smoothly as they worked together, it still took them nearly four hours to finish the job. But in the end, they left no visible trace of their presence. And their handiwork was lost in the landscape.

When they finish, Jeep say, "Let me test it for you, Grikkl."

He points his trusty compass at the just-repaired tear. The needle spins around in a crazy fashion. He points it in the opposite direction, and it still spins around non-stop. Jeep marches along the entire stretch of their repairs, never taking his eye off the compass needle. It never slows down.

"There's plenty enough energy here on this side of the barrier to make my compass go catawampus. Looks like the leak is gone."

Outdoors, as they worked in the direct sunlight, Jeep can better observe that Grikkl really doesn't seem to be solid. Once back in the cozy cavern, Jeep asks him, "Why do you shimmer like that? Are you transparent?"

"No. My body's just as solid as anyone else's. It looks weird because of something special the krindle can do. Someday you could shimmer, too—once in a while."

"I've never seen anyone act like that. People can't do that."

"It's possible for humans too. Rare but possible. What's uncommon about me is how I walk, don't cha know. It's something I developed to protect my mangled foot."

"You mean the way you bounce?"

"Aye. Think about the way people stand up—they *push themselves up* from the floor. People are stuck on the ground, heavy, you see?"

"Gravity you mean?"

"Exactly so—gravity. It pulls people down. Me, I'm a student of the laws of levity. Gravity has its place, but levity…"

"Isn't that about laughing?"

"Aye, that's one form. But there're others you've yet to come across. Some scientists consider it to be the opposite of gravity, to be anti-gravity. But I call it levity—the power to elevate any situation. The trick is to balance gravity with levity—and become one with the forces of nature."

"I can see gravity holding things in place, but I can't see what levity does. And you're telling me it's just as important? I don't get it."

"Levity does its job even if it looks like nothing much is happening—by keeping gravity in check. Don't just look with your eyes, Laddie. There's always more going on than the eye can take in. Lots more. Today we fixed a tear your eyes couldn't see. But it was there just the same. Right? Don't be deciding what's real just by what you can see."

At bedtime, Adah makes Jeep an exaggerated frowny face. "I sure am going to miss you. I'm going away for a while."

"But I just got here. Can't you put it off?"

"I must go, it's time. Every year I visit the land where babies live before they're born. All day I hug their innocent spirits and sing to them—every single one." She laughs lightly, as she pretends to rock an infant.

"They like my songs, too—like you do. I fill their wee hearts and spirits with binkles. After they're born they bring that joy along. Every child starts life with a krindle that works and a heart full of binkles, offered to everyone they meet."

"Surely you know how sad it makes me that you're leaving. Please stay—I need you."

"I know, indeed I do. I won't leave until tomorrow and you'll see me again in about four months. But Jeep, the work I do is most important—and it makes me happy beyond words. About twenty of us take turns with this task. I must do my part—the others count on me. It would be a terrible day if some babies were ever born without binkles.

"Two of my friends, Layda and Taloo always take their turn the same time I do. It's not all drudgery. The three of us make a merry crew, that's for sure.

"Taloo's such a gossip—better than a newspaper. Whenever something interesting goes on, somehow he manages to be there—like when the queen of the elves learned to water ski behind a dolphin.

"He's hard to describe and can do weird things with his body—it stretches. He's a character, by any measure. Trust me, it's never dull with Taloo around.

"Layda loves music more than anything. It's her special gift, one she's eager to share. I learned many of my songs from her—but she sings much better than I can. Layda fancies herself a muse[3], and who's to say she isn't?

---

[3] *The Muses - In Greek mythology, the nine daughters of Zeus, who presided over the arts and sciences. Calliope (heroic poetry), Clio (history), Erato (love poetry), Euterpe (music and lyric poetry), Melpomene (tragedy), Polyhymnia (song and speeches), Terpsichore (choral song and dance), Thalia (comedy), and Urania (astronomy)*

"As long as I've known her, she likes to travel around sending melodic inspiration to musicians, composers, dancers, and singers. Once in a while, I'll hear someone sing or play a tune, and I'll say to myself, 'Layda's been there.'"

"Don't be sad while I'm gone. You and I are never separated, even when we're far apart. Our hearts are connected, so when your heart is happy I know it. When you're sad I know it. And when you're afraid I know that, too. I can tell what you feel."

"I'll be alright, Adah, just a little sad without you."

"Only apart from me, but never truly without me. Send me a binkle and I'll know."

"Where's that place with the unborn babies? Is it even on this planet? And I'm assuming you're talking about their spirits, not the babys' bodies."

"Glad you caught that. Where I'll be is very close and very far, since it's not in the same dimension as this one. You know something about different dimensions already. Here, where Grikkl and I live, is a place where several other dimensions connect up with your human world."

"Could I ever be able to go to that baby place with you?"

"Who can tell?" she beams with her twinkling warmth. "But now, I want to sing."

Adah sings a song he never heard before—one she sings to the unborn babes. The melody takes Jeep back to babyhood and all its loving feelings. He experiences himself as a tiny baby once more, held snugly by his mother.

No words, no ideas, just feelings—happy ones. Everything feels good—there is no cause for fear or sadness. All is well. All is taken care of. Just love. That's what he feels. All he knows. And that is enough.

Afterward, Jeep confides to her, "I miss Mom all the time. But I'm going to see her soon. Chris is taking me. He promised."

"Wonderful! A mother's love has its own magic. Let her know how much you love her, and let love do its work."

Finally, Jeep can bear to speak of favorite memories from when his mom was still home—like cooking together, and walking barefooted on the wet, sandy beach. He is glad to be able to talk about those special memories with someone—even though such happy times don't happen anymore.

"I know it's hard, Jeep. I know—but they're not gone for good."

And the next evening Adah is gone. While Jeep misses her, with Grikkl and all the critters in the cavern, he is anything but lonely.

Too soon to suit him, it is time for Jeep to return home. Grikkl hands him a package of faduki cookies and hugs him goodbye. *That's a first with him. I wonder what's changed.*

"I can't wait to come back. I keep getting better at finding binkles." *And now I know I can get back again.*

"Good, Laddie, no doubt you will. But in my opinion, you're ready for something more challenging. I've got an important assignment for you—a test."

"I don't like tests. Do I have to?"

"Would you be more eager if I called it a quest? A significant trial of your courage and ingenuity?"

"But it's the same assignment either way, isn't it?"

"Aye. To my way of thinking, you've got enough spunk to do it."

"I'll do my best."

"That's all I'm asking. Your task is to convince Mr. Slade on Market Street to donate the ravine that runs along the zoo's west side. That property would make a great natural sanctuary for some of the animals. And the zoo needs that additional space."

"An adult would have to do that. I'm only a kid."

"Tut, tut… The first challenge on any quest is how eagerly you embrace the mission. You must take on the task willingly and without delay. Otherwise, you failed before you begin.

"No excuses. No logical reasons why it won't work. That kind of thinking closes the door to a *seemingly impossible* outcome."

He points at Jeep. "What say you?"

"Like the knights of yore, I will go forth to seek my destiny."

"Right answer, Laddie. And I'm confident you're the right person for the job."

Grikkl nods sagely, as though he knows more than he is telling.

In farewell, Lulu speaks directly to Jeep's heart, in ways more trustworthy than words can ever be. Jeep is perfectly happy as he holds her and fondles her fur.

Like before, her cuddling is the last thing on his mind in Grikkl's cavern. And the next morning he wakes up in his own bed back home, still dreaming of her.

A package of faduki cookies rests on one side of him. And MeToo is curled against him on the other.

CHAPTER 12
THE DISTURBING
VISIT TO ELKHORN

On the eagerly awaited day, Jeep and Chris drive nearly five miles into the countryside, before they arrive at the hospital. Jeep was too excited to sleep the night before. The closer they come, the happier Jeep gets—and the sadder Chris gets.

"Chris, there's so much to tell her. So much catching up to do. Have you been telling Mom about me?"

"Yes, I tell her. But Jeep, don't expect too much. She's not the way you remember."

"I know. But she's still my mom. I know she loves me."

"She's not herself. It's another kind of sickness. That's why she's at a mental institution, not a hospital."

Jeep doesn't understand the difference, but it will become clear soon enough. *I only care that I'm about to see her, to hug and kiss her. This nightmare will be over.*

Chris turns off the main road. Elkhorn Institute's sign is painted in brown letters on a sky-blue background. All Jeep can see beyond it is the tall fence that cuts the facility off from the rest of the world.

As a guard at the gate stops them, Chris answers his questions. Then the gate opens to let their car in.

Once inside the tall fence, a wall of evergreens is planted so closely together they block Jeep's view until the car almost reaches the main building.

His first sight of Elkhorn gives him the willies. It is large, dark, and uninviting—like a military fortress. The doors and windows have bars on them. He can't find a single note of cheeriness in the entire scene.

From the moment he steps out of the car, Jeep feels chilled. The person who signs them in at the entrance acts more like a guard than someone on a medical team.

"It feels cold here—almost like a jail," he whispers to Chris. "Maybe it's so yucky to make people hurry to get well so they can go home." His words seem hollow bravado.

Once they're signed in at the front desk, Chris hold back. "I'll wait here. Jeep, you have to do this yourself. Take all the time you need."

"You sure? I thought you were going to come."

Chris shakes a decisive no.

An orderly guides Jeep through the long corridors. Along the way, they pass many shuffling people with far-away expressions, obviously patients, along with others wearing medical garb, going about their responsibilities. Nobody smiles or seems to notice them passing by.

At Helen Parker's room the orderly holds the door open for him and walks away. The room seems as dreary as everything else Jeep has seen so far. Helen's home was decorated with cheerful pictures and needlework that she made.

This room lacks any of her personal touches, except for a bulletin board that shows recent pictures of him and Chris.

Jeep sees a woman slumped sideways in a padded armchair. She appears to be much smaller than he remembered his mom being, like she's shrunk. The faded hospital gown hangs loosely enough to exaggerate her skinniness. And her face lacks expression of any kind.

He calls out, "Mom, mom… it's me, Jeep."

No reaction. No recognition. Her eyes are open without focus, without showing any interest in his being there.

Jeep tiptoes closer to her. "Mom!" He almost yells—as if getting louder would make her pay attention.

In that instant, the truth hits him with devastating force. *Ohmygosh, that woman resembles mom, but doesn't have her personality. I've pictured this moment so often, but not like this.*

To say that Jeep is disappointed isn't even close. He feels dejected, despondent, devastated, and miserable, not to mention broken hearted. His eyes sting with unshed tears, and his shoulders sag in defeat.

173

No! This can't be happening! Nothing I've waited for is going to happen. I have to go, to get out of here.

Yet he also wanted to tell her, "I still love you and think about you every day."

What can I say to this woman so far-away? I can't find the right words—any words. Maybe binkles... but how?

Jeep drags a chair over close to hers, so he can face her on the same level. *It has to be enough for me to touch your hand, even if you can't tell.*

He clings to the simple, trusting love he feels, and aches for it to reach her. Not knowing anything else to do, he just sits beside her, loving the woman who doesn't know he is there.

Jeep holds both her hands with both of his. Hers are warm but limp. Around her slender wrist is fastened a bracelet that hospitals use to identify patients. It says HELEN THOMPSON. Jeep idly rubs his finger along the letters.

"Yup, it's Mom. It says so right here," he mutters. *It's odd that something as small as an ID bracelet hangs so heavily from your bony wrist.*

Jeep lightly strokes her delicate, unmoving hands, taking what comfort he could from touching her. He loses track of time, as he sits as quietly as she does.

After a while he starts to talk. Not like he expects her to hear him or to react. Just because it is familiar to talk to her like he used to.

He speaks in a rambling way of a time when they went camping together. Not like a long hike or anything, but getting to sleep in a tent.

"We stayed up late and watched the stars come out. It was glorious! The whole universe on full display. You and I ate snacks in our sleeping bags—not like something we'd ever do at home. Who'd care if we dropped crumbs? Just be a treat for some bird or squirrel to come upon.

"We tried to tell scary stories. But first you started laughing, and that got me laughing too. We kept laughing so hard because we couldn't consider the 'scary' stories anything but funny."

Those were the good times. Now as he tells his mother of the almost-forgotten outing, that special camp-out is real all over again, because of sharing it with her. *Maybe Mom can't remember it. But I can—for both of us.*

He keeps on talking. About half an hour after he arrived, a nurse comes to guide him back. Her name tag says, "Helga Schmidt, R.N." She has a grandmotherly way about her and seems sincerely concerned about him.

"This has to be a shock for you." She nods toward Helen. "She never responds to any of us, either. Or to her husband."

"Do you think she'll ever get better?" he asks.

"I've seen stranger things—so it's always possible. Only time will tell."

Jeep idly pats his mother's hand, as reluctant to leave as he'd been to stay when he first came. He bends over and presses his lips to her cheek—not quite a kiss.

He holds that position for longer than the situation warrants. He's is not quite sure what to feel—or if he dares to feel anything at all. This is his beloved mother. The person he has always loved. Whose affection he's never doubted. And now she is only a shadow of herself, unable to give or receive love at all.

A tear leaks down the side of his nose, silently betraying his disappointment. He smears it away with the back of his hand. He makes a final effort to kiss her goodbye.

In that instant, Helen's arm swings out widely, and her hand pulls at Jeep's earlobe. The next moment her arm collapses into the non-moving flesh it was before. There's nothing to indicate it had ever moved.

She pulled my earlobe!!! She pulled my earlobe! Jeep silently screams, as his heart filled with joy. *She recognizes me! She knows it is me!*

"Did you see that?" Jeep asks the nurse.

"Yes, but it doesn't mean anything. Just a reflex. It's not like she intends to reach out to you."

Jeep is definitely not persuaded. He knows with unshakable certainty that his caring presence and touch have somehow reached her. And she responded through touch as well—the only way she could.

Although his mother did nothing more, Jeep gratefully received her message. When he was very small, her gentle pulling on his earlobe had a special meaning for them. It was her private, silent signal to say, "I love you, Jeep."

While sitting at her side, he'd done his best to accept what couldn't be endured. But now, that gesture tells him that she isn't entirely gone. Something of her remains—even though speaking isn't possible.

Jeep silently promises both of them, *I know you're in there, somewhere. I just have to find some way to reach you. I'll be back and won't give up until I find it.*

But misery sets in when Jeep gets home. Except for her pulling on his earlobe, the whole trip is too painful for him to think about. He grieves for his mom, and he grieves for himself as well.

All the months of stored-up hopes were crushed in a moment. Her expressionless image is forever tattooed in his memory. Wave after wave of sadness keeps forcing itself into his mind.

I never doubted that she'd be home soon. Seeing her like that shows me I've been hanging onto a childish daydream. It's not going to happen.

Jeep cries non-stop, being unable to break it off. *I can't help myself. My life might have been miserable, but until today I had hope. Now that's dead. She's not the person I remember. Who knows if she'll ever leave that awful place? When Chris told me Mom's crazy, I didn't think it could be so bad. It's bad, alright—worse than I ever imagined.*

MeToo sticks close to him, showing why he was named MeToo in the first place. A dog's affection is a wonderful pick-me-up, but there's only so much a dog can do for heartbreak.

Hour after hour, Jeep's tears fall. *No, please no! My heart can't stand any more.* Chris is gentle with the boy, and finally calls Louise and Anna to come lift Jeep's spirits.

The girls sit quietly, knowing words can provide little comfort with suffering so deep. But despite their kind efforts to make him feel better, Jeep cannot find any relief.

The next morning Jeep is out of tears, but is too worn down to handle school or being around other people. Chris agrees.

"You can stay home, but only if you stay in bed and rest."

"That's all I want to do, anyway. I need to be by myself."

Mostly Jeep sleeps the day away. MeToo cuddles against him and bathes his face in doggie kisses, now and then.

Jeep is abruptly awakened mid-afternoon by MeToo's growls. With fears rising, he grabs his baseball bat and tiptoes into the living room. The intruder is another dog.

 "Cerberus! What are you doing here?"

"Adah sent me with an important message."

"How'd you find me?"

"Puh-leese! That's what I do! Deliver the mail."

MeToo wants to know, "If you can talk to dogs, why don't you ever talk to me?"

"I never even thought of it. We've always gotten along just fine without needing that."

"Yea, sure, but you'll talk to him."

"I'm sorry—forgive me. I'll talk to you, too—promise."

He treats MeToo's growl as grudging agreement.

"MeToo, meet Cerberus. And Cerberus, this is MeToo."

They sniffed each other in the way dogs do. Then both sit and wait for Jeep to read Adah's message.

My dear Jeep,

I told you our hearts are connected, and I can feel your deep sadness. Your mother is in great danger. You have the ability to rescue her—as long as you do not doubt the strength of your love and the power of your krindle.

Dry your tears, my sweet. For her sake, you must be strong and move soon. Use the special mirror I've sent with Cerberus to look into the faces of those who surround her. It will reveal whether the person is true or serves Uuglash.

Binkles, Adah, A Priestess of a Different Sort

Jeep studies the front and back of the small round mirror that Cerberus brought with the note. It isn't remarkable in any way that he can tell.

When he holds it up to his tear-streaked face, he looks the same as usual. Holding it before MeToo, no difference. Cerberus, no difference.

Maybe that's how it works. Probably only Uuglash's followers look any different in it. But what am I looking for? How can I tell?

Jeep scribbles a note for Cerberus to deliver to Adah. That done, Cerberus sets out for places far away and is gone in a twinkle.

Adah's note knocks Jeep out of his misery quick enough. *She's far away, but she knows I'm suffering. Adah told me what I need to know. My mom needs me!*

Jeep announces to MeToo, "Enough moping! I've got a rescue to arrange." He sets to thinking.

With all the locks and guards at Elkhorn, getting her away won't be easy. I must analyze every fact about that place and devise the course of action most likely to succeed. Already, I feel like I'm Sherlock Holmes. Jeep the Detective is on the case.

After school, the sisters come by to check on how Jeep is doing. Were they ever surprised at the change! Jeep's suffering is gone—replaced by a determined detective.

Jeep tells them about Cerberus coming and shows them Adah's warning and mirror. The girls can't figure out how the mirror works either.

Anna and Louise want to help. After considerable discussion, they come up with a three-part strategy.

First, Jeep will spend time at Elkhorn so he can use the magic mirror to size up the staff and learn how things work around there.

Second, they use the information he gathers to devise an escape plan.

Third, they'd get his mother away from there somehow.

Jeep recalls a spy story where a person was seen so often that everybody stops noticing him. After a while, he becomes the "invisible man."[4]

Jeep thinks he can do the same thing at Elkhorn. By going to see his mother almost every day, he figures the staff will get so used to him being around they'd ignore him.

Whatever he can learn about the staff, or schedules, or building layout is bound to help their planning. The three of them need to make sense of the facts about his mother's care so they can decide the best plan of escape.

Jeep tells them, "This is a spy mission. If there's one thing I've learned from organizing all that truffle data I collected, it's how to arrange facts. I'll gather intelligence about Elkhorn, and we'll figure out what to do with it together."

They are in full agreement.

Chris is very relieved to see Jeep in a happier frame of mind. Jeep already decided not to tell him about the warning—at least not yet.

Instead, Jeep tells him, "I guess I really had a hard time accepting the truth. I know you tried to warn me, but I had to see her for myself."

---

[4] G. K. Chesterton – "The Invisible Man," a short story

"The way she is now is hard to deal with. I know. It's heartbreaking to see Helen like that. Now you can understand why I tried to keep you away. It was for the best."

"Yea, what you did makes more sense now. I won't be so upset the next time I go see her."

"You mean you want to go back there? You can't be serious!"

"I think I should. I don't want to run away from this and I'll get used to the idea much sooner if I spend more time with Mom."

"But Jeep, there's nothing you can do for her."

"I know. That's why I have to go back, don't you see? Just to be near her. Is it OK with you if I go see her every few days?"

"Of course not! There's sure to be more misery for you. Haven't you suffered enough?"

"But I have to do this. Can't you understand?"

"I'm well aware of how hard it is to go there and visit her. To see her just staring into nothing. It's tough. And not likely to help her anyway. Think what you're asking."

"I've been thinking about nothing else all afternoon. You could be right…"

"It doesn't make me happy to be right about this. I care about you too much to see you suffer."

"It's just for a little while after school," Jeep pleads.

"I can't take you out there," says Chris, as though that put the kibosh on Jeep's request.

"I know and don't expect you to be along. I've already got that part figured out," says Jeep, being careful not to sound too eager. "It's not too far for me to bicycle—when the weather's good."

Though uneasy about it, Chris assumes that Jeep will soon tire of going. "I guess it's worth a try. I'll give permission—as long as your chores don't suffer."

Already, the first part of The Plan is ready to roll.

CHAPTER 13
HIGH-STAKES
NEGOTIATIONS

Jeep doesn't want to do Grikkl's assignment—not even a little bit. As far as he's concerned, the whole idea about him getting the zoo property is a big mistake. So, over the next few days he works out one excuse after another so he won't have to do it.

In the end, he had to admit to himself that he's scared. He doubted himself, he doubted he could succeed.

What made Jeep go ahead anyway is his certainty, *I'd rather face Mr. Slade than have to face Grikkl with the knowledge I didn't even try. At the very least, I must give it my best shot since Grikkl trusts me. Besides, it's a quest.*

Jeep calls to make an appointment. The secretary can tell she's speaking to a child and refuses to take him seriously. She tells him, "Mr. Slade is not available," with a note of finality.

Jeep gets the same treatment the next five times he calls, even though he disguises his voice.

Part of him wants to say, "Well, at least I tried," and be done with it. But the part of him with spunk knows there has to be another way.

He cleaned himself up as though going to church and heads to Market Street. Jeep tries his best to look and act businesslike, knowing that he fools no one.

The sign near the elevator says: Slade Investments - 1037. He gets off the elevator on the 10th floor. The door at 1037 opens into a fancy waiting room with dark paneling and little lights over each of the framed paintings. Even he recognizes that means they're expensive.

A middle-aged secretary sits by the door. "I'm here to see Mr. Slade," Jeep says, trying to sound businesslike.

She is no more obliging in person than on the telephone. Her eyes inspected him up and down without approval. "Do you have an appointment?"

"Is Mr. Slade in today? Does he have time to see me?"

Jeep is no dummy. *Answer a question with another question. Make her do the talking.* Too bad—she isn't a dummy either. Cementing her sour expression, she sent a question right back.

"Young man, what are you up to? Mr. Slade is very busy man…"

She is interrupted by the buzzer. "Miss Kublic, please come in here."

She gives Jeep a warning look and hisses as she leaves. "Don't touch anything."

When Miss Kublic returns, Jeep is sitting in the chair next to her desk with a cheery smile. *Still no dummy, I know a smile's my most persuasive move—besides, it keeps people guessing.*

"You still here? What do you want?"

"An appointment with Mr. Slade, please."

She shakes her head no, then does her best to ignore him while she stares rigidly at her computer screen and types away. Ever so often she glances in his direction and frowns.

For the next hour, Jeep sits with the I-want-you-to-like-me expression on his face, like he has nothing more important in the world to do (which is true).

"I want you to leave, now," she finally snaps.

"Of course, happy to—as soon as I get an appointment."

"I can't do that."

"And I can't leave without one." He pauses to think, "Maybe I don't need an appointment—if you'll let me see Mr. Slade without one."

She's one step away from being polite to me.

"You're not going to make this easy for me, are you?" Her face relaxes a trifle.

"I'd like to go away right this minute, honest. But I *have to* see him. I doubt either one of us wants me back here tomorrow to start all over again."

That does it. Worn down by his positive persistence, she folds.

"You win. I'll let you in, but only for five minutes. Then you promise to leave without a fuss, right?"

"That's all I want."

First round for me, but that's just the warm-up. I've got to do better with the boss.

Miss Kublic ushers him in, with a comment to her boss that the boy will only stay a few minutes. The inner office is deluxe, with dark, heavy polished furniture and shiny brass accents.

Mr. Slade is a slender, silver-haired man who speaks and moves with clipped efficiency. Never a wasted movement. His clothes fit him like they were made for him, and everything in his office screams "expensive."

Not surprisingly, he is on guard and impatient to get rid of Jeep.

Jeep wastes no time. "Mr. Slade, I'm here to speak for the animals. I understand you own the property next to the zoo. I want you to donate it to the zoo. The animals need it."

"Young man, that land is not available. We're getting ready to build there."

"I know, that's why it's so important that you act right away—*before* building starts."

"It's out of the question, there's a lot of money involved."

"Can't you at least think about it?"

"Absolutely not. Nothing to discuss. Why would I even consider what you're asking for?"

"I'll give you two reasons." Jeep counts on his fingers. "One, it's hard to build along a ravine, so you'd be smarter to put that factory on flatter land somewhere else.

Two, all that loud construction noise will frighten the animals for a long time. Then operating the factory will make a racket once it's built. No question, they'll suffer from all that noise.

"They're already having a hard time being so crowded up as far as possible from where your factory will be. Besides, I guess this must be three, wouldn't that gully make a nice animal enclosure without cages?" He finishes on a pleading note.

Mr. Slade doesn't even take time to consider Jeep's arguments. "Young man, I'd have to be crazy to take your request seriously. You don't know the first thing about business."

"That's true, sir. But I do know the first thing about animals."

Mr. Slade reflects on that for a moment. "Really? Perhaps you do... Then maybe you can tell me what's wrong with my parrot. His feathers keep falling out and he doesn't talk anymore."

Mr. Slade gestures across the room. A large parrot slumps on its stand in the corner of the office. It sits so still Jeep didn't notice it was there until Mr. Slade mentions it.

At one time the bird must have been covered with bright, beautiful feathers. But there weren't many of them left. Instead, pimply, pinkish skin shows through what few feathers remain. Its head droops on its scrawny neck.

It only takes Jeep a glance to see that the bird is going downhill fast. Jeep approaches the bird, still without a clue about what to do next.

I'll fail, sure as shooting but at least Grikkl will know I tried. Whoa… Now's not the time for giving up. Something's definitely wrong—maybe I can get the bird to tell me.

Jeep turns to Mr. Slade. "Sir, I think I know something about his problem. If you will please go and bring me a large magnifying glass, I'll be able to give you an answer shortly. What's his name?" J

Jeep really doesn't need the magnifying glass, but he does need to get Mr. Slade out of the room for a minute.

"Rubens," says the man as he left.

Jeep approaches the bird. "Rubens, I want to help you if I can. Do you know why your feathers have fallen out?

"Sure, I pulled them out myself," answers the bird, almost proudly.

"But why? What could possibly make you do that to yourself?"

"If you must know, Mr. Slade is driving me insane. I can't stand it anymore."

"But if you continue, you'll get really sick or worse…. That's not smart."

"Whatever it takes," Rubens answers with a shrug. "I'm prepared to kill myself—commit parrotcide—if I have to."

"Surely not! That can't be the answer!"

"I've run out of choices. Since he's driving me crazy, why shouldn't I act like a loony bird?" Rubens asks, in a way that doesn't sound like he is crazy at all.

"That's pretty extreme. Isn't there another answer?"

"Can't think of one."

"What's he doing to you that's so bad? He looks like a reasonable man."

"Mr. Slade has a mighty fine music system in here—the best. Up until recently he played the classics—you know, Mozart, Handel, Beethoven. It was wonderful! That music fed my spirit—made me soar inside.

"Then about a month ago he starts playing Country and Western songs all day long. Can you believe it? Country and Western—all that yammering about misery and heartbreak! It's terrible, I tell you—it's more than a bird can bear!"

Jeep is dumbfounded. "That's it? You don't like the music? You'd commit parrotcide over music?"

"Now you're getting it."

"Can't you learn to like Country and Western?"

The bird's horrified expression makes Jeep drop that idea.

"OK then. What if I could get the music back like it was? Would you stop this foolishness and let your feathers grow back?"

"That's all I want. That blasted Country and Western music gets me depressed."

"Everything else is OK with you? What about food? Anything else you'd rather have?"

"Now that you ask—I'd rather eat Livermore Parrot Treats."
"I'll see what I can do—but you've got to stop this nonsense. Deal?"

"Deal."

For the first time, Rubens takes a good look at Jeep. "Who are you, anyway? Dr. Doolittle making a house call?"

Just then, Mr. Slade returns, carrying a large round magnifying glass.

Jeep uses it to look the parrot over up close—peering into its eyes, feet, and feathers. He tries to act like he actually is a doctor in the process of making his diagnosis.

"Mr. Slade, we're lucky we got to Rubens in time—a very serious case, indeed. The worst I've encountered. I know what's troubling your bird. With your help, we can soon have him healthy again."

"Well, out with it, then."

"It's about parrot psychology. Birds are very sensitive and I'm afraid Rubens' will to live has been weakened. He requires healing surroundings to rebuild his enthusiasm for life."

"Yes? so…"

"In my experience, music can help to speed up recovery. Certain music increases their vibration level and animation. And that's a key to health. Animals respond well to the classics. So, I recommend that you play a steady diet of Beethoven, Chopin, and Mozart for him.

"You think that's it?" Mr. Slade asks scornfully.

"Certainly not! There's a psychological factor as well, which I've taken into account. However, if you follow my advice, I'm confident Rubens can become a healthy bird again very soon."

"I doubt that music can make much difference. But I'll play the classics, for a while, anyway. This better work, young man."

Jeep and Mr. Slade talk further about Ruben's overall health, the changes in his diet, and the importance of soothing sounds for healing.

Jeep is smart enough to know it's best to leave on a high note. He gives a wave to the bird on the way out.

"Goodbye, Rubens."

As he leaves, Jeep's final words hang in the air, "Think about donating the zoo property. I'll be back."

Since Jeep is already gone, he doesn't see Mr. Slade's stunned expression when the parrot responds, "Goodbye, Jeep—Be seeing you."

When Jeep phones the office three days later, Miss Kublic treats him with respect and impatience.

"Mr. Slade is most insistent. He needs to see you right away. Can you come at four o'clock today?"

"This afternoon will do fine."

"Very good, Mr. Parker. He needs to know what you did to his parrot."

When Jeep arrives, Miss Kublic smiles cordially at him. "Mr. Slade can see you now, Mr. Parker."

As Jeep steps into the inner office, Rubens calls out, "Hey, Jeep, what's new?"

The parrot hasn't grown any new feathers yet, but it now stands tall and alert. The cheerful strains of a Mozart symphony filled the room.

Although the bird looks much better, the man looks far worse. Mr. Slade's clothes are rumpled and his gaunt, weary face betray his lack of sleep.

Mr. Slade is impatient to take charge. "What have you done to Rubens? He's driving me nuts."

"What do you mean?"

"I'm trying to tend to business here. It requires all my brain power, but he's messing with my mind. How can I get any work done with his non-stop interruptions?"

"What's he doing?"

"Rubens hasn't stopped chattering since you left. I suppose it's good that he's bouncing back. But the darned bird refuses to give me a moment of peace or quiet. And he's bossy."

Jeep shifts into his doctor mode, "What's he been saying? And more importantly, why does it bother you so much?" He turns and winks at Rubens.

"He keeps repeating I should just give the land to the zoo. You put him up to it, didn't you?"

"Of course not! How could I? He must have overheard what I said to you. I'm as surprised by all this as you are."

"Like I'd believe you," the man says with sarcasm.

"Still, there must be more to it than that. If you don't like what Rubens says why not just ignore him?"

"Ignore him! Ignore him! Don't you think I'd ignore him if I could?"

The gentleman certainly wasn't as confident as he was at their first meeting. But in the battle of nerves, he came in second to a bird.

"If you must know, Rubens was my father's bird. My father raised him and trained him. Rubens sounds just like my father. You expect me to ignore my own father?"

Mr. Slade collapses back into his chair, as though his over-wrought emotions consumed the last of his energy.

"I see." Jeep nods and taps his chin as though in deep thought.

"Rubens hasn't been talking much for a long time. But now he won't stop. It almost seems like Dad is speaking to me from the grave."

A haunted expression clouds the man's eyes, and it seems like his logic has slipped a bit, too.

Jeep takes his time, nodding wisely, "So you really think your own father is talking to you… through Rubens?"

"It seems that way, doesn't it?

Jeep makes a shrewd guess. "Tell me, do you think your father would want you to give that land to the zoo if he were here?" From the man's reaction Jeep can tell he'd hit a nerve.

"Wasn't that your father's land in the first place? You inherited it from him, right?"

"Sure, that land is part of what he left me. If he were alive he'd probably let you have it."

Rubens squawks, "Give the land to the zoo," like he's been saying all along.

The man jumps in alarm. "Make him stop! Please, oh please! Make him stop."

Jeep's eyes hold Mr. Slade's gaze for a long minute. "You know there is a way to get Rubens to stop saying that, don't you?"

"There is? Can you make him stop?"

"No, Mr. Slade, I can't. Only *you* can make him stop."

"But I don't know how! You've got to make him stop," the man wails.

Jeep speaks with the kind of soothing voice someone uses with an upset child. "Of course you do, Mr. Slade. Just – do – what – he – says," as though it is the only intelligent solution.

"Yes, I suppose you're right. That's reasonable. Why didn't I think of that?"

"Give the land to the zoo," Rubens squawks once more.

"OK, OK! The land goes to the zoo…, if I never have to hear that again! Now make him stop."

Some decisive action is required, but I'm not sure Mr. Slade is up to it at the moment.

Jeep points at the phone, "Why not call your lawyer and tell him to draw up the papers?"

Mr. Slade's instructions to his lawyer are firm as they nail down detail after detail. He ends the phone call, "Get those papers over here for my signature right away."

Jeep whispers his thanks to Rubens while Mr. Slade is talking on the phone.

The bird answers, "Any time… Just listen to that Mozart, will you—heavenly."

After he hangs up, Mr. Slade sits aback and stares at Jeep a long time. "Young man, maybe you and old Rubens outfoxed me. But I'm starting to feel better about this.

"What's all my money for if I can't be foolish with it now and then? Let's just call this 'Be Kind to Animals Day,' alright?"

Jeep opens his mouth to say something, but nothing comes out.

So, he just grins. *I can't wait to tell Grikkl.*

And in due time, Mr. Slade is as good as his word. He didn't stop with donating the ravine to the zoo. He brings together engineers and zoo experts to design a first-rate wildlife habitat for the animals. Some of them can live together without cages in a natural setting.

Mr. Slade's team even figured out an observation area built into the rocky side of the ravine. Visitors can watch the animals close up, without disturbing them at all.

Everyone agrees the whole thing is marvelous. Even better, Mr. Slade pays for the improvements.

When the plans are complete, Mr. Slade holds a press conference to announce what's in store for the zoo. His impressive designs are covered by the local newspapers, radio and TV. Politicians try to take credit for it, but Mr. Slade praises Jeep as the mastermind behind the whole thing.

Jeep's picture appears on the front page of the newspaper above the words, "Local Boy Expands Truman Zoo."

As part of the dedication ceremony zoo officials announce Jeep's appointment to the Zoo Board as the official Animal Spokesman. Little do they realize his special qualification for the job.

CHAPTER 14
THE TRUFFLE DISASTER

Jeep works until twilight in the park nearly every day collecting truffle data. Because of the need for secrecy, he couldn't do his work when other people are near enough to watch him.

He happens to be there one day when a woman walking her dog sits down on a bench nearby. She unhooks the dog's leash to let him run free. Then she tosses him a ball, that it fetches and returns.

One of her throws is very wide, and the dog loses sight of the ball. He chases around before digging at the base of a tree. That's where the dog finds something that he brings back instead of the ball.

What happens next freezes Jeep's blood. The woman does the worst thing he could've imagined!

"Wow! Truffles! Right here in our park!" she yells with excitement. She runs to the hole where it was found and digs around until she finds some more.

To anyone who comes along, she hollers, "Hey, look what I found! Truffles!"

She might just as well have yelled, "Gold!" The secret is out—and what comes next resembles a gold rush.

Jeep calls Chris with the horrible news.

Chris leaves work so they could watch what happens next. They can only sit by helplessly, as the heartbreak of their dashed dream plays itself out.

Rumors spread fast. Within hours the park is crawling with truffle hunters, eager for their share of the find. The discovery makes the news. That attracts even more truffle hunters. Over the next several days, their years of work gets destroyed, or is enjoyed by strangers.

Jeep can't be sure which of their patches might have survived undisturbed. But if he checks any of them soon, he'd call attention to where they are.

Chris and Jeep know that despite their careful secrecy their scheme has failed. Their ship came in—but not for them.

They'd have to start over again—probably somewhere else. That is, if they had the heart to face so much hard work again.

The truffle disaster brings another form of gloom down on them full force. Their cherished hopes for financial relief are dead.

Worse yet, Chris loses his nerve. Until that happened, neither of them realizes how totally Chris has been counting on truffles to save Helen and his finances.

During the days that follow, Chris looks empty and emotionally haunted. He calls in sick as often as he bothers to show up for work. For, indeed, he is sick—sick in heart.

And if he can't get past his depression, physical ailments will surely follow. Jeep looks after him like a parent cares for a sick child.

One good thing, I don't have to do any more truffle chores. Now my afternoons are free to go to Elkhorn.

Jeep's mind sometimes wanders off to fret about the bullies when it should have been on his schoolwork. He feels he needs to do something—so he won't be such a wimp.

Yet Grikkl's warning about inviting in evil leaves him few choices. *How can I deal with bad guys without playing by their rules?*

Jeep uses Adah's mirror to see if Merve sets it off.

Whatever the mirror can detect, apparently Merve doesn't have it.

Maybe he isn't so bad. If only I could get him to talk to me without being so nasty.

After weeks of pondering on the puzzle, Jeep remembers something. *Mom used to say, "I can't be upset while I'm eating." How about Merve and me eating together? Maybe then he won't be so mean.*

Jeep raids his savings, but figures it's for a good cause.

On Saturday, Jeep phones Merve, "I need to talk to you. Meet me at the Ice Cream Palace at 4:00 today. I'll pay."

A puzzled, but reluctant Merve agrees to come. He knew that whatever Jeep was up to, at least there'd be ice cream.

Jeep is seated in a booth waiting when Merve arrives. "I've already ordered."

"What's this all about, Jeep the Creep?"

Before Jeep can answer, the ice cream arrives. He ordered The Gold Digger, which is dramatic and huge. The super-duper $27 sundae has twelve scoops of ice cream plus four gooey toppings, nuts, whipped cream, and, of course, cherries (five of them) on top.

Their waitress delivers The Gold Digger with the drama usually reserved for a Thanksgiving turkey (and it's nearly as big). She proudly fusses over her grand showpiece. Though he won't let on, Merve is impressed—and eager to dig in.

"Gosh, if I'd known it was this big, I'd have told you to bring your friends along. Mind if we eat before we talk?" Jeep asks.

What could Merve say but OK? Besides, that much ice cream will melt if not eaten immediately. Each boy digs in, working hard to demolish the tasty mountain.

Jeep breaks the silence. "This chocolate-chip mint, mmmmm… I'll bet it's the best flavor here," as he waives around a half-eaten spoonful.

"Can't be," mumbles Merve with his mouth full. "It's the peach."

"Could be…, I'd better check," says Jeep, as he dramatically scoops a bite of the peach ice cream and pops it in his mouth.

He doesn't swallow it though. Instead, he makes a great show of swishing it around in his mouth, like he'd seen a wine taster do. Unlike the wine taster, however, he swallows it in the end.

Finally, his verdict—"You're right, peach is better."

Merve watched this over-dramatic taste test so closely he'd forgotten to keep eating. "Peach is best—I won." he crows.

"Oh, we don't know that yet. We've got to compare scoop by scoop, flavor by flavor. We can't be sure peach is the winner 'til we check them all."

"I suppose," allows Merve with his mouth full. "Maybe if we both try the same flavor at the same time?"

So, they each take a bite of the cinnamon-raisin. "Not bad," says Jeep.

"I don't like it," insists Merve.

The boys get into a rhythm—scoop, taste, vote. Lemon custard rates two "pretty goods."

When they taste butter pecan, they say, "Naw!" at the same time, and with exactly the same expression of distaste. They burst out laughing.

Chocolate ripple is rated "blah" compared to double chocolate. So, bite by bite, the two boys taste their way through the platterful of ice cream. They work against time, determined to devour the mountain before it melts into a puddle.

On some flavors, Jeep and Merve agree; on others, they don't. But either way, they're having fun together. Now and then, one of them says something silly and they'd laugh some more.

By the time the winner is picked they agree on one thing—they can't eat another bite. Yet nearly a third of it remains uneaten.

Jeep mimics an announcer like he's seen on TV, "And the winner is (long pause). But first I'd like to thank the judges—Merve McCoy and Jeep Parker. Let's hear a round of applause for the judges."

Both boys make an exaggerated bow, which is hard to do when sitting down, and while also making the fake applause.

Jeep starts over again, "The winner is… But folks, you know what a hard choice it is. And all the contestants are deserving. We're sorry that there can be only one winner. Let's congratulate all the others that came close—maybe next time."

Jeep really hams it up, and Merve goes along with the silliness. "The winner is…, drum roll please… strawberry cheesecake! Let's hear it for strawberry cheesecake!"

Again, the fake applause, with both boys doubled over laughing at themselves.

When the last of the ice cream is cleared away, Merve remembers he still doesn't know why he came, and tries to return to his tough-guy role.

"So, what do you want me for?"

"I want to figure out why we can't get along."

"That's easy. I don't like you—or your friends."

"Why's that? You don't know me and I don't know you. So why us?"

Merve prefers action to words and doesn't want to talk about this stuff. But Jeep refuses to waste the moment.

"Maybe you didn't like me before—and that's OK. We know each other better now. Look, we just ate a mountain of ice cream together. We're not friends, but we proved that we can get along. And I had a good time with you."

Merve doesn't exactly agree, but at least he listens. Jeep continues, "Wasn't this pleasant? Isn't it better than fighting?"

"What are you up to, Jeep? I think you're trying to trick me."

"No Merve, that wouldn't be nice. I want us to be nice to each other."

"Is that all? Just be nice? I'm not buying it. Be nice…, be nice…," he mimics.

"If you think you can…."

"Sure, I can. If I want to, I can," Merve insists.

"Great! I knew you could, and I thank you."

"For what? What are you thanking me for?" Merve asks suspiciously.

"Why, for saying you'll be nice, of course. You're going to stop picking on the little kids—that's real nice."

"I didn't say that. Why should I?"

Jeep shakes his head as though Merve isn't making sense.

"C'mon, admit it. It's not much fun anymore. You and your buddies could have a lot better time after school doing something you like. Not just picking on the little kids."

"Like what?"

"Maybe sports? Maybe a hobby? Lots of choices—all of them more enjoyable than picking on kids who can't defend themselves."

The two of them speak of sports, and games, and after-school activities. In the end, they found they have more than a little in common.

Somehow, Jeep and Merve move away from open hostility and add something new—cooperation.

Did that solve everything? Of course not. But ice cream and binkles together are a good first step.

CHAPTER 15
DETECTIVE WORK
AT ELKHORN

In order for The Plan to work, Jeep needs to show up so often the staff at Elkhorn get used to seeing him around. He follows the same routine day in, day out.

After school, he rides to Elkhorn on his bicycle, rain or shine. At the gate, he stops long enough to visit with the guard on duty. Before many days pass, the guard waves him through without the usual paperwork.

Jeep always takes the time to chat with the nurse he met on his first visit (named Helga Schmidt) as he arrives. She'd report about his mother's condition. Although that never changes, her efforts were kindly meant.

The first problem for him to solve is how to get his mom out of her room. *I can't spend all my time in there, since that would keep me from looking around like I need to.*

Jeep asks for help from Mrs. Schmidt. "Mom needs to get out of her room. I want to take her outside so she could get some sun and fresh air."

"Great idea. I know where there's a wheelchair that's not in use."

They dig it out of a dusty storage room. Then she shows him how to steer it about smoothly and the safest way for him to lift his mother in and out of it.

From then on, Jeep explores Elkhorn inside and out. He takes his mom outside to sit in the sun, unless the weather is bad. Although she doesn't speak to him, he can see her body responding to the warmth and being near growing things.

Jeep talks to her nonstop, as he points out all the people and happenings along the way. It doesn't take long for the staff to grow accustomed to their comings and goings.

True to his mission, Jeep leaves and returns to the main building by as many different routes as he can find. He always brings a book along so he can read aloud to his mother, in the hope she's listening. He only chooses happy stories—just in case.

Jeep is surprised to find he actually likes to be at Elkhorn. *At first, I thought it was cold and unwelcoming here, but not so much anymore. This place is swarming with people—some who need help, and some who want to help them. All of them could use a binkle.*

Jeep's friendliness (a new skill which he considers an essential part of his disguise) turns out to be easier than he expected. Soon he knows almost everybody's name and waives "Hi" to patients and staff as he wheels his mother past. They brighten up a bit, and many called back, "Hi, Jeep, How's it going?"

"It goes to show, there are binkles to be found everywhere—when you're looking for them," he tells Anna and Louise as he reports the events of the day.

Although their outings look like nothing more than a casual walk, Jeep never forgets why he's at Elkhorn. His eyes and ears notice details about whatever they pass. His apparently idle chitchat collects facts that might be useful when the time comes. In the evening, he'd debrief (the spy word for reporting what he found) his friends.

Sherlock Holmes would have been proud of this team. Jeep, Anna, and Louise make elaborate notes about the staff's routines and schedules. They map the building and the grounds with clearly marked entrances, exits and surveillance cameras. Gaps in their data are dutifully filled in as Jeep brings back more intelligence.

 Louise and Anna take it upon themselves to help cover for the long hours Jeep spends at Elkhorn. They do some of his cooking and cleaning tasks so Chris won't find out how much time Jeep is spending there.

Jeep keeps Adah's magic mirror in his pocket so he can check out each person he sees. After a few tries, he figures out the best way to use it. He holds the mirror up in front of his face, and looks at the person over his shoulder as he walks away from them.

The problem is, everybody looks normal in the mirror. It doesn't show me anything unusual about anyone. So, is everyone at Elkhorn OK?

 He has a chance to find out sooner than he expected.

Late one afternoon, he sees the retreating back of someone he doesn't recognize. Quickly he uses the mirror. The person's image is normal. But the entire face of the mirror is blood red.

Ohmygosh! That's what I've been waiting to see. He's Uuglash's man!

The cold hand of dread (that's a really bad case of fear) grabs Jeep's stomach. Almost immediately, the suspicious man is gone.

Every detective knows staying alert often spells the difference between life and death. Jeep is determined to be even more alert now that he knows how to recognize what he's been looking for.

I spotted one bad guy. Probably he's not alone. Just to be on the safe side, he keeps the mirror cupped in his hand. Jeep checks everyone with it—even those who'd already passed the mirror test.

With added caution, Jeep spends even more hours roaming Elkhorn, watching for signs of Uuglash's men. He pushes his mom and the wheelchair everywhere that isn't locked. The one place he has yet to explore is the basement.

The next time Jeep catches sight of the suspicious man, he's carrying a tray of small bottles near the nurse's station. The mirror confirms the worst—all red.

Jeep asks the nurse, "Who's that? I haven't seen him before."

"Oh, that's Del Dexter. He works in the lab."

"Where's that?"

"Down in the basement."

Jeep gulps.

Jeep never had an excuse to go to the basement since it isn't on any of the routes in and out of the building.

No avoiding it now—I've got to check it out. I'll just take a quick look-see. So, I'd better leave the wheelchair upstairs. But without my usual "cover" There's no excuse for me to be down there.

Jeep sets the brake on Helen's wheelchair when he parks it on the stair landing. He takes a quick look around—the coast is clear. He gathers his courage and tries to calm his racing pulse.

He starts chanting to himself, "Be strong—I think I can, I think I can, I think I can…"

Jeeps takes the first step down, pauses and listens; then another, pauses and listens; and another… He shivers, feeling colder with each step. He finds himself walking slower and slower, step by deliberate step. He scolds himself for being a scaredy-cat.

I've been watching too many scary movies. There's probably nothing down here to be afraid of.

When Jeep finally reaches the bottom, only silence greets him. And there's no going back.

CHAPTER 16
A BOLD RESCUE
ATTEMPT

The narrow corridor stretches ahead of him, from the bottom-most stair to a single point at the far end. It looks vacant from one end to the other under the glaring light fixtures that dangle from the ceiling.

The doors along both sides of the hallway are closed and apparently locked. The flip-flop of his own footsteps, echoing along the concrete floor, is the only sound Jeep hears.

Each step makes Jeep more jittery. *Calm down, now. You're just going to look around. You'll be back upstairs in no time.*

Jeep only finds one door open along the hallway. He peeks around the doorway. It's the lab. He steps stealthily into the brightly lit room, looking about in all directions. Nobody is there. *See, no problem—nothing to worry about.*

It looks like a laboratory is supposed to look. Tall shelves of stainless steel vessels, sparkling glassware, and scientific paraphernalia fill the work stations. The counters are covered by complicated equipment. A partly open door leads into another lighted room on the far side.

Jeep hears steady buzzing and bleeping sounds from a large machine that stands near the middle of the room. A tangle of twisting tubes and pipes stick out of it, and colored lights blink above a row of dials.

A screened-off area on the left side of the lab is devoted to housing lab animals. The arrangement of cages and tanks contains about twenty rats, rabbits, frogs, and small monkeys. Jeep wanders over to where he can peer into their cages.

He is so caught up watching the animals that he doesn't hear someone enter the lab from the far room.

 "What are you doing here?" demands a harsh voice.

Jeep jumps. Then his heart freezes, as he turns and looks into the scowling face of Del Dexter for the first time.

"I heard there were animals down here. I wanted to see them," Jeep answers in his most innocent voice.

The man moves close, right up to Jeep's face. "I don't believe you, you little sneak. I've seen you around, don't think I haven't. What I want to know is what you're up to."

"Up to…?"

"You can just cut out your innocent act. I said, I've been on to you for a while. You aren't fooling anybody."

"What are you talking about? I just come to Elkhorn to see my mom."

"Down here? Sure, you are—and my name is the Tooth Fairy. I told you, I already figured out *what* you're doing. What I still don't know is why."

"Why do you think I'm doing anything? I certainly never saw you around before." *How did I give myself away? I've been so careful.*

Del isn't buying it. "The binkles, dummy. Do you think I couldn't spot them?"

"Binkles?"

"There usually aren't very many binkles around a depressing place like this. Right after you start hanging around they start showing up all over—just like a bad smell."

"Binkles? What do you know about binkles?" *I'm surprised to find anybody who even knows what they are, especially someone as disagreeable as him.*

"That's my job, little boy. I'm an expert on them. I'll bet I know more about binkles than you do."

I doubt that—it can't be. "If you don't mind my saying so, you don't look like a person who even knows what binkles feel like. You're too much of a sourpuss to be a binkle expert."

Dell laughs a nasty laugh. "Feel them? No, I wouldn't want to feeeeeel them. Not me. I'm more like a farmer. I harvest them—put 'um to better use."

"What do you mean, harvest? I had no idea… I thought most people just felt them."

"Most people? Most people?" Del's face wrinkles up like he'd swallowed a bug. "For them that's probably true. But I'm not like most people! Way ahead of them, I am. I know enough not to waste them."

"Waste them? I don't understand. They're just something you feel when you're happy."

"Told you I know more about them than you do! Admit it." Del crowed like he'd scored a touchdown.

"Looks like you do, 'cuz this is all news to me. Binkles are for feel-good energy."

"That's not the half of it, kid. We've got a system—with science and everything, see. I know how to harvest that energy for more important purposes."

"Really? You really think so? Binkles don't work that way."

"Maybe not for you. But like I said, I'm a pro." Del gloats, then laughs again at Jeep's baffled expression.

"See that machine over there?" He points at the large machine with blinking lights, "It's made special to capture binkle energy. Collects it from the patients here—like milking cows, see."

"No way!"

"When you started hanging around and doing your little aren't-I-nice tricks, those meters shot way up. And you didn't think I'd notice. Stupid kid, you didn't even suspect I'd be able to tell."

"That's amazing! I never thought it would show."

"Of course, that increased my binkle collection rate—so it's not all bad."

Jeep walks up to the flashing machine and taps on the largest dial. From the way Del tenses up, Jeep can tell he doesn't like him doing that.

"This machine can do all that?" He touches it some more in other places. "Impressive!"

"Buzz off kid. Don't mess with the machine. It's none of your business."

"This contraption pulls the energy right out of the patients, does it?" as Jeep keeps handling the machine all over. His detective mode is cranking now.

"I suppose that's why the patients' ID bracelets are so heavy. Links them up to this fancy dandy machine, right?"

"So now you know."

"Very clever! I never would have guessed. Never. And nobody else knows either, right?"

"You've got it, kid." Del's tone has shifted from bragging to threatening. "So now you see why I've got to stop you. Can't have you messing up a good thing."

"I see you're smarter than I thought."

"Told ya. Now scram."

I've gotta get out of here. He's dangerous! Jeep's hand nervously fiddles with his trusty compass, and pulls it out of his pocket without thinking. Out of the corner of his eye he sees the needle spinning round and round as fast as it can go. Just like in the Chamber of Ancient Wisdom.

Hmmm. Strange, there must be a lot of binkle energy in here. So, it must be the machine.

Jeep asks, "One thing I don't understand. What do you get out of this?"

"Power. I control everybody who lives here. Besides, you don't think I spend my whole life down here working, do you? I get my pay-offs, believe me."

"Sounds like you've got it all figured out." Jeep wants to as him more questions, but Del's menacing attitude makes getting any more answers unlikely.

"Stupid kid! You're messing with the wrong people. You made a big mistake coming here. Your last mistake."

He's dangerous—this is exactly what Grikkl warned me about. Only two things I know—don't get scared or do anything evil. But Grikkl's only advice for me was to trust my krindle. And here I am, without a clue what that means.

Aloud Jeep says, with more willpower than he feels, "I'll put my trust in the krindle."

"Stupid kid. You don't deserve to live."

Jeep does his best to shut out Del's ugly words. Instead, he repeats the chant, "Trust the krindle, trust the krindle, trust the krindle...."

Del yells threatening insults at him. Yet, for reasons Jeep is unable to understand at the time, or to explain later, he can barely hear them. The more Del screams, the farther he seemed to move away from Jeep.

Del throws whatever he can reach at the mumbling boy (glassware, jars of chemicals, lab instruments). Not a single object hits its mark. But it sure makes a racket, as it smashes to the floor. *Boy, I'm lucky his aim is so bad.*

Alarmed by his inability to hit the boy, the color drains from Del's face. He backs away, then turns. In two long strides, he reaches his desk and pushes a large red button. Doing so seems to take the last of his resolve and energy. He collapses into his desk chair.

Time seems to stand still for Jeep and Del. Each seems incapable of breaking free of their hypnotized standoff. But ever so slowly, something starts to happen, starting along the floor.

The room darkens, as a billow of dark smoke begins to coalesce on the floor. The smoky swirls slowly gather until they take on a very whispy human shape. The form gradually becomes denser and darker, becoming less indistinct with the accumulating smoke.

A sense of deep hopelessness and grief sends shivers of terror through every cell of Jeep's body. He senses a despair so dark that it blots out all feelings of goodness or hope. It sucks out anything in him that could have made him feel strong or resolved.

Before long, in the midst of the swirling smoke, stands a mammoth, bald-headed man enveloped in a black robe. He stands between Jeep and Del. His head almost touches the ceiling, but his legs are still merged into the still-swirling dark, smoke on the floor. The apparition's presence spawns a cold blackness that chills the heart and sucks the air right out of the room.

Jeep finds it harder and harder to breathe. But he also knows the panic he's feeling reflects his alarm at what's happening, and is not simply fear.

It is terrifying! The apparition's spiteful and merciless face glows against the darkness he carries around him.

"Uuglash, I assume?"

Uuglash glares down upon Jeep as though he is a nasty little insect. "Not amusing," he hisses. "You are a foolish child and have no idea what you've blundered into. You're nothing more than a lowly worm in my presence."

Jeep merely nods in petrified agreement. It's obvious that he is no match for the dark one.

"If you'd dare to oppose me, you'll learn about pain—pain beyond enduring. I'll smash you!"

Uuglash grows ever larger and darker as he speaks, which makes Jeep feel as if his own body is shrinking. He is indeed becoming insignificant.

"Trust the krindle, trust the krindle…" Jeep quietly mumbles.

Uuglash is triumphant. "Beg, you worm. Beg for your life. You have lost! Totally and completely lost! And not you alone. Your helpless mother sits at the top of those concrete stairs. She cannot survive her wheelchair crashing down. Do I need to describe how she's going to look at the bottom? I can, with the flex of my finger—this finger—make that happen."

"No! You mustn't!" Jeep cries out.

"And how will you stop me? You can't!" Uuglash's form pulsates as a triumphant and merciless snicker plays through him.

Too frightened to disagree, Jeep keeps on mumbling. "Trust the krindle, trust the krindle…"

"You dare to resist me? It's over!"

Jeep cannot speak or hit upon any way to respond. The weight of those damning words bespeaks doom and resignation. It's over.

Uuglash points both hands, with his index fingers extended, directly at Jeep.

"Viday!"

That gesture sends a bolt of malevolent energy to zap the helpless boy out of existence. The air crackles with electricity. Sparks fly.

Although Jeep can see the bolt coming toward him, he never feels the burning whack of it that he expects. Instead, he notices that Uuglash, like Del before, seems to be moving away from him in slow motion.

The next moment, Uuglash himself writhes on the floor, felled by some unseen force. Time stands still, as Jeep's feet are rooted to the ground, and he cannot comprehend what is happening.

The evil one slowly rises and yells at Del, "Help me finish this troublesome snoop."

Del remains fixed to his desk chair, incapable of taking action.

Uuglash scowls. "Later for you. Coward!"

Uuglash then speaks to Jeep, every word dripping with spiteful venom. "I suppose that's a trick Grikkl taught you. Not bad, really. But it won't save you. My power is infinitely greater than yours—or his.

"Did Grikkl tell you how I almost destroyed him? Foolish, foolish little gnome… What can either of you do to stop me?"

His arrogant, hateful words sting. Jeep wants to argue, to defend Grikkl, but all he dares to say is, "I'll trust the krindle."

But one of Uuglash's nasty comments stings Jeep more than the rest. His mother is in grave danger, and Jeep doesn't doubt Uuglash can easily topple her wheel chair and send her crashing down the basement stairs.

And it is all my fault. My behavior put her in grave danger—worse than before. And now I can't save her. I wish Grikkl was here to help me about now.

Unable to do anything in her defense, Jeep just keeps chanting, "Trust the krindle…, trust the krindle…, trust the krindle…."

Those words further enrage Uuglash. His shadowy form grows darker still, and it shakes with anger. Once again, Uuglash points his hands and extended index fingers at Jeep, as he directs a burst of evil energy.

"Viday!" The air sparkles and crackles.

This time, when the blast of energy again crumples Uuglash, Jeep isn't caught totally by surprise. *Got to get out of here and save Mom. Not much time to escape before they get me.*

Jeep turns the water in the lab sink on full force. Then he directs the faucet hose at the humming, blinking, binkle-sucking machine. As the water hits it, electrical flames shoot from the machine in all directions. The stream of water shorts it out.

Pop! Crackle! Zzzt... The sparks keep flying around the room, bouncing off the shiny steel surfaces.

All the bright flashing lights and loud popping sounds scare the lab animals. Their frantic caterwauling adds to the racket and confusion. Jeep releases each cage latch as he dashes along the row of lined-up pens and cages.

As he opens every cage he yells at the already terrified critters, "Run, run, run!"

Jeep grabs a nearby broom and swings it around, forcing the terrified animals to run toward Del and Uuglash. *Gotta keep them busy until I get to Mom.*

The panicking animals create pandemonium in their rush toward freedom. The last thing Jeep does before running from the lab himself, he shoves over a tall rack of glassware and lab equipment. What a commotion!

The hubbub and crashing glass echoes down the corridor as Jeep gallops along the seemingly endless hallway. His rush of fear-fueled adrenaline plays tricks with his mind, with what he is hearing and seeing.

He can't be sure that all of the crashing noise is behind him. The echoing noises could have been coming from either end of the hall. Maybe from his Mother's disastrous fall.

Like in a slow-motion movie scene, Jeep feels himself running and running, but not getting any closer to the stairway. His feed against the unyielding concrete, but without delivering much forward motion. *Am I getting away or stuck in some invisible tether of Uuglash's making?*

Ahead he thought he could hear the sounds of something crashing down the steep concrete stairs—accompanied by the softer sounds of ripping fabric and smashing flesh. Jeep's dread of his mother's wheelchair tumbling down is foremost in his mind.

Is this to be the disastrous outcome of all my efforts to get her home? Or were those horrible sounds just the venomous notion that Uuglash planted in my thoughts?

Jeep feels enormous relief when he doesn't come upon his mother's crumpled body at the bottom of the stairs. But he can't be sure it is real, either. Is it just what he wants to see, rather than the horror he had imagined?

Jeep can no longer trust his own senses. Instead of calming relief, more fears erupt. *Is this a trap to slow me down, fooling me into thinking I've made it?*

Jeep scurries up the stairs, two at a time. At the top landing his mother sits unmoving in her wheelchair, just as he'd left her. She is totally unaware of their peril, having long since escaped from all fears, into her own distant world.

Jeep reaches forward and brushes his knuckles against her cheek. Senses deeply programmed into him recognize this, his first human tie. *It's Mom, alright—not an illusion fueled by Uuglash's tricks.*

In that moment of unmistakable recognition, that fear loses its icy grip on him.

But they aren't safe yet. Jeep pushes the wheelchair as fast as it is capable of going. But it wasn't designed for speed. He rushes frantically forward.

Where can we escape Uuglash? There's only one place…

Jeep gasps for air as he runs. He's desperate for a long, deep breath. That urgent need arising from his body triggers a memory—one which suggests an uncertain escape plan. Risky? Yes indeed—but also a glimmer of hope.

Jeep stops abruptly. He walks to the front of the wheelchair and gently bends across his mother's body. His heart aches to see how shrunken and fragile she is. Yet her frailty is precisely the key to their escape.

He lifts her up just enough for him to slide under her in the wheelchair. Now she is sitting on his lap, cradled in his arms. Jeep wraps his arms tightly around her. Only by stretching his neck forward can he bring his head next to hers.

His fingers can barely touch the cord around his neck, so he must lean even farther forward. His fingers clutch at the medallion, and he wiggles around until both of his hands can grasp it. Jeep holds his breath as all his thoughts are focused on Lulu.

This has to work—there's no time for a Plan B.

(Blip)

Jeep plops onto Grikkl's sofa in his cozy, underground home. *Hallelujah! We made it!* His mom still rests in his arms, unaware of their moving across space.

Their arrival disturbs Grikkl. His reaction is amazing in its own right since nothing ever manages to catch him by surprise. The wise gnome always acts as though whatever happens is exactly what he expects. Not this time.

There's no way a slumbering woman falling out of nowhere could've been expected—even by Grikkl.

As soon as Grikkl sizes up the situation, he says with urgency, "We must get this bracelet off right away. Uuglash's team can't follow you into this space. But it's unwise to let them know where she is."

Heavy wire cutters can't cut through the bracelet. "That means there's a potent spell on it."

Grikkl starts to chant. After several minutes, the bracelet falls off her wrist. But he continues chanting until the ID bracelet melts into a shapeless lump. Even then, Grikkl isn't satisfied that it is harmless.

He calls Cerberus and places the steaming lump in the dog's pack.

"You know where it has to go." With a nod, the dog leaps forward and vanishes.

Grikkl explains to Jeep, "The evil curse on it may be broken, but it mustn't be permitted to pollute our energy."

Grikkl is wonderfully caring to Helen. Once he's able to assess her condition, he tells Jeep, "Although I'll do my best, dark magic has been used on your mother so long… We'll just have to see."

Jeep totally trusts Grikkl and never doubts the gnome's ability to completely cure her. For days, Grikkl spends most of his waking time at Helen's side. Lulu is just as attentive, sending her a steady stream of affection.

Jeep is surprised when Heather and Yawn actually move from the place where they always sit, to snuggle against her. Judging from their past inactivity, it's likely to be a permanent move.

When he gets a free moment, Jeep sends a message to Anna and Louise, carried to them by Cerberus.

Louise and Anna,

I got Mom out of Elkhorn. But it was dangerous—a close call. Had to abandon all the plans we made. We're at Grikkl's, but Mom is still real sick.

Don't know how long I need to stay here. Will tell you more when I can. Thanks for your help. It worked.

Jeep

The girls are both equally delighted their weeks of hard work paid off. They send back a note with just one word, "Hooray!"

CHAPTER 17
THE TRUFFLE
SECRET REVEALED

The next day, Grikkl tells Jeep, "What I need to tell you should be discussed in the Chamber of Ancient Wisdom. But you and I can't leave your mother alone for long. In ordinary times, you wouldn't be ready for what I must explain to you. But these aren't ordinary times…

"You need to understand what was really going on yesterday. There's a good explanation for why you escaped from a situation that could so easily have ended badly for you.

"You know best," Jeep mumbles with foreboding, since Grikkl's grave manner makes him fear the worst.

"Remember when Dexter threw things at you? None of them hit you. Strange, isn't it? Then later when Uuglash sent his evil bolts at you – Viday! That didn't hit you either. Remember?"

"Of course—it's puzzling. I was waiting for something terrible to happen to me. They were too close for their aim to be so bad."

"Exactly so. What saved you isn't their poor aim. They saw their shots *couldn't* hit you, couldn't harm you. That realization really scared Dexter and Uuglash. For they understood that as powerful as they are, they're no match for you."

"Huh…, come again?"

"Strange—since you assumed you were no match for them."

"But I wasn't, I'm not. What happened, then? It doesn't make sense."

"No, it doesn't make sense. You'd consider it impossible if you hadn't seen it happen with your own eyes. But it did happen—or your mother and you wouldn't be here."

Grikkl's bright eyes twinkled as he nods in her direction and holds a long-drawn-out pause.

"Despite Uuglash's much greater strength, you managed to do something rather remarkable."

"I survived?"

"Aye Laddie, but not only that. You were able to use a new power—one you didn't have before."

"But I didn't do anything at all because I didn't know what to do."

"That's probably what protected you. You weren't too sure of yourself. Not over-confident."

"That's for sure! I had no confidence at all!"

"Uuglash got back exactly what he dished out. You reflected the destructive ray he sent to you back to him—in exactly the same amount."

"But I couldn't have done it, Grikkl. I don't know how to do something like that. Besides, it happened too fast."

Grikkl idly strokes his beard, "Seems that way, doesn't it? But you did do something. And what you were able to accomplish is more important than you had any way of knowing."

"Huh? What?"

"You trusted your krindle. Remember?"

"But I only said that. I didn't know how to do it, or even what it meant."

"Doesn't matter. Just saying it was the right choice for you to make. The only choice that could've saved you. All the faduki you've been eating has been developing your krindle much faster than usual.

"Besides that, your binkle-finding activities charge it up. Yesterday all that effort paid off. When you needed the krindle's unique super-charged power it was there for you."

"But it didn't happen like that! Honest, I was there."

"Jeep, the krindle did it…, whatever you think. If I had the sense to do what you did back when I met up with Uuglash, I'd still have a whole foot."

"No, Grikkl, no… Why can't you believe me? I don't even know what it means."

"Sure, I believe you. But what I'm telling you is true all the same. What happened when you were face to face with full-blown evil shows how the krindle can work when circumstances are just right.

"Let's back up a little. Remember us talking about my shimmering? You see me shimmer, but I can't see it myself. There's an energy field on the outside, around me. I can look right through it without ever seeing it's there."

"Yea, I suppose. So?"

"That same kind of force protected you, too. The krindle caused a temporary energy field a lot like that to form around you. Puny, I'll admit. It wasn't strong enough to hold very long. Good thing you made a run for it when you did."

"How? I still don't understand."

"When conditions are right, and the binkles are strong enough, the krindle is able to form an energy barrier around somebody. It's invisible but as solid as steel. That's what turned back Uuglash's blast of evil."

"But why?"

"There's no cruelty in you. So, the evil energy they sent your way had to bounce back to where it came from—to Uuglash."

"You're telling me my krindle can do that without me doing anything?"

"Exactly so. Your krindle worked. Amazing, isn't it?"

"Amazing is right! And a little scary."

"The force that protected you is called 'tablixx.' That's the name of the energy barrier. It's a marvel you experienced it already—you being so young."

"Good thing! Because without it I didn't stand a chance!"

Grikkl's devoted nursing starts to rebuild Helen's strength. As she slowly clears out the cobwebs of her mind, she notices bits of what's happening around her. As days would pass, she steadily adds more simple activities—feeding herself, brushing her teeth, playing with Lulu.

Helen's speech is like a small child's, and she still can't put ideas together. A puzzled expression never leaves her face for long.

Jeep keeps watching for any signs of her cheery self. But they are mighty slow in coming. *I'm sure it's only temporary. She'll be better soon. She's just got to be.*

Several days after Helen's arrival Grikkl tells Jeep, "We need to go tell Chris how Helen is doing. No doubt Elkhorn already told him she's missing. I'm sure he's worried about her."

Once it is dark, Jeep and Grikkl walk to the roadway, where they catch a taxi. Jeep asks, "Why don't we just go by magic?"

"Why rely on magic, when a taxi will do very well?"

Then he drops his voice and looks a bit sheepish. "If you must know, there's another reason—more personal. We're going into your world. I have a rough time holding myself together for long out there. I need to save every bit of my energy for meeting with Chris."

"Oh, yes. The kittens hendrini problem?"

"Exactly so. I can't stay away from home long without fracturing."

Jeep could picture the gnome's strange shattering. "That would confuse Chris even more then him wondering what I'm doing with someone like you."

 "That's probably the least of what we will talk about. Just don't let me lose track of the time."

Chris comes to the door when they knock. He is puzzled. "Jeep, what's going on? Why aren't you in bed? And who is this person with you?"

Before Jeep can open his mouth, Grikkl takes charge. In an exaggerated gesture, he bows so low his head almost touches the floor. Then he marches into the living room with Jeep close behind. Grikkl holds up his hand to forestall any more questions.

"Good sir, we've come with important news about your wife, Helen."

Mentioning her gets Chris even more desperate for answers. He explodes with questions, revealing how worried he's been.

"All in good time, sir, all in good time."

Grikkl gestures for all to be seated. Then he speaks to Chris.

"Your wife was held under a disabling spell that robbed her of her wits and kept her sick for some time. Young Mister Jeep's courageous efforts rescued her from a cheerless nightmare. I'm happy to say, she's improving now under my care."

Grikkl tells Chris as much as he can, without revealing the hard-to-believe parts (which kept the story from hanging together). That version of the facts leaves a lot of puzzling gaps.

Chris doesn't get all the answers he asks for. But it's more than he had before (and probably as much as he could handle).

Grikkl admits, "It's too early to make predictions about her recovery, Chris. But given Helen's depleted condition, I'm hopeful. What I'm doing for her now offers her the best chance to recover. Maybe the only one.

"Have I your permission to continue?"

Chris nods—probably more from his head spinning than from sensible agreement. But Grikkl acts like the discussion is finished and Chris has agreed.

Then abruptly changing subjects and proceeding in a chattier tone, Grikkl says, "Too bad about your terrible experience with the truffles. Would it surprise you to know that I'm an expert when it comes to cultivating truffles?

"Really?" Jeep asks in surprise.

"How did you manage that?" Chris asks.

"Aye, Chris. I'm a gnome, you know. Gnomes and truffles share a lot of history together. We both dwell under oak trees. Living together for thousands of years has taught gnomes a thing or two about what makes truffles thrive. I know exactly what it takes to grow them."

"Don't tell me you know…?" Chris manages to sound both disbelieving and eager to hear more at the same time.

"Indeed, it's tricky—but no mystery to me. Young Jeep described how hard you both worked to figure it out. Impressive effort. Would it bother you for me to come right out and tell you the tricks?"

"Tell me! Were our experiments on the right track?"

"You almost had it. But there's a missing piece you hadn't solved. Without that, the other answers couldn't accomplish very much."

"I've gotta know," Chris insists impatiently.

Grikkl turns his head toward Jeep and winks. He said under his breath, "He doesn't even think it's strange to have a gnome in his living room, or for one to be a friend of yours—he's so obsessed with truffles."

Grikkl leans closer to Chris. "Don't worry, I'm getting to that. Truffles grow because of the relationship between the truffle fungus and the oak roots, which benefits them both. The roots provide water and carbohydrates for the fungus. At the same time, the fungus helps the roots absorb minerals from the soil.

"The scientific term for how they grow together is mycorrheza (myco, fungus, and rheza, roots). That part is well known. I'm sure you're familiar with it.

"What's not known is that there's a third life form involved that's every bit as important—a particular bacteria. It has to

236

be there for the other two to be able to grow and nourish each other. When that bacteria aren't present, no truffles. What you still needed to figure out relates to that bacteria."

"What bacteria? How…?"

"Hold on. That's a conversation for another day. Don't worry, I'll explain it all. Right now, Jeep and I need to get back to Helen."

Grikkl starts to leave, then pauses at the door and speaks as though the words are an afterthought.

"Before we go, I have a proposal for you. Young Jeep here, has done me a great service—which I can never fully repay. In gratitude, I beg you permit me to do a good turn for your family.

"I'd like to offer you the use of charming cottage located near where I live. This isn't an ordinary house, if you get my meaning. It's in my oak forest, which grows truffles just as you imagined it could happen."

"You mean it produces truffles now? Already? That takes years!"

"Exactly so—but gnomes are patient and long-lived. These truffles are well established. There are more than you can imagine, enough for a comfortable living. Help yourself to them. Sell as many as you can gather. Money won't be a problem anymore."

Grikkl's generous manner turns businesslike, "However, you must guard the information I share with you. Tell no one else. How you come by the truffles you sell must remain our secret. Is that acceptable?"

"I promise—no problem there."

So, a deal was quickly settled, handshake and all.

At the doorway on his way out, Grikkl adds, "I'll let you know when Helen can move to the cottage. OK?"

A stunned and disoriented Chris nods. Grikkl had that effect on people.

"I trust it's acceptable to you if young Jeep stays on with me to help care for his mother."

Chris nods again. Then he glances at Jeep, as though noticing his presence for the first time. "How do you fit in all this, Jeep?"

"I'd love to explain—but the kittens…"

"Oh yes, the kittens," said Grikkl with urgency. "We must go."

He marches out before Chris can say another word. Once they're on the street, Grikkl takes Jeep by the hand—and this time they travel by magic.

Helen improves bit by bit, but she isn't close to being her old self. Her emotions have been turned off. She is neither happy nor unhappy. She can speak in simple sentences and listen when people speak to her. But she doesn't understand much of what they say or mean.

Saddest of all, she can't binkle. She can't sort out the meaning of what she hears or sees—let alone feel the caring.

Several weeks into her recovery Grikkl reports, "Jeep, I've done everything I can for your mother. But her emotional links are gone and her krindle's broken. She suffered too much damage at Elkhorn for me to fix it all.

"She will improve and can live with you and Chris again. But she won't ever be like you remember her."

"Are you certain? Isn't there anything else? If we gave it more time… I'm sorry. I've tried and tried—even with my best knowledge and magic. There's nothing more to do."

"That can't be true, Grikkl. We got her out of there—it can't end like this." *It's not fair… Not fair,* Jeep cries inside.

Grikkl suffers deeply from his failure as well. Was this to be another victory for Uuglash after all? How much is due to his failings? Is it a sign of him getting "old" and losing his edge— past his prime and effectiveness?

Grikkl tells Jeep, "It's time to get you, your mother, and Chris into that cottage as soon as we can. Your lives will be better because you're together again—even if it's less than what you hoped for."

The cottage is charming, just like an enchanted cottage tucked among the old oak trees should be. It is surrounded by a white picket fence, overgrown with trellised roses and ivy. Less apparent are the abundance of truffles growing beneath the surface.

It doesn't take many days for the three of them (plus MeToo) to settle into their new home. Helen is able to cook and clean around the house, but she does it in a rather mechanical way.

Jeep still goes to the same school, so he gets together with Anna and Louise often.

Grikkl patiently teaches his truffle secrets to Chris and Jeep. Enough of the pungent and valuable knobs are ready to be gathered for Chris to build a successful truffle business.

Since he no longer works at several jobs or away from home, he isn't worn out and discouraged any more. And he can give Helen all the assistance she needs.

MeToo learns how to be a truffle dog. Lulu moves in with the family and becomes a truffle "dog" as well. Very soon life settles into a routine that's OK, although considerably less than wonderful.

Chapter 18
A Magical
Tea Party

Weeks later, came the day Jeep was secretly waiting for—Adah is back. She already knew from Grikkl how things stand with Jeep's mom. And she knows Jeep's family is living in the truffle cottage.

As soon as Adah sees Jeep, she stretches out her arms to grab him and then holds him close. *I want to hold onto this moment as tightly as she holds onto me.*

After the two of them catch up somewhat, she tells him, "There's news that must be told at the Chamber of Ancient Wisdom. Grikkl was just waiting for my return."

Without delay, the procession of Cerberus, Grikkl, Adah and Jeep trudge through the passageway. Once they get settled in, Grikkl holds Jeep's gaze for a long time. *Something important is up.*

"Jeep, what I'm about to tell you is disturbing. I don't want to add to your pain, but truth must be served."

"I can take it—if you think it's something I should know." "Good Laddie, you're strong. Remember how upset I was that

I couldn't heal your mother? I sensed there must be more than just an illness at work on her. Indeed, there was. He exchanges a meaningful look with Adah, but she says nothing.

"I was able to learn, don't ask me how, that your mother was marked for Uuglash's evil schemes even before she went to

Elkhorn. "Before she got sick, she used to be extra high energy, a walking binkle fountain. Not hard to spot that much special energy, either. Don't you agree?

"Oh yes, everybody could feel it."

Grikkl continues. "The day she took sick, she went to a job interview. The person she met was a recruiter who recognized what she could offer. But he wasn't thinking of jobs. He saw her as a binkle source. Like Del Dexter, he (along with others like him) played their part in the whole ugly, devious scheme.

He gave her something that messed with her wits, pushed her over the edge. But I don't need to tell you about that part—it's better not to dwell on it.

"And once she ended up at Elkhorn for treatment, well—you know the rest. They milked that precious life force out of her for a whole year. It's a crime, a heartbreaking crime."

Tears trickle from Jeep's eyes. "I needed to know. My poor mom." Adah holds him close as the tears fall.

Once he got a grip on himself, Adah says, "When your mother gave you your compass, it was really a symbol for you. She wanted you to know you're never lost when you have a compass."

"I remember. I think about her words whenever I use it."

"But now it's your inner compass that's keeping you from being lost."

"You mean the krindle? asks Jeep.

242

"Smart Lad," Grikkl replies, with a nod toward Adah. She just beams at Jeep in the special way of hers.

"Now on to more pleasant matters." Grikkl declares, as he holds out his open palm.

"Give me your medallion, Jeep."

"Why? You're not taking it away from me, are you?" He fumbles with the cord around his neck as he unties it. This was the first time he has taken it off.

"Certainly not. You have more use for it now than ever. Let me show you something." Grikkl points at the symbol on the back.

"See that? It's a very old, top-secret symbol only a few understand. It stands for Eight Foot Pygmies. Get it? See the 8 – backward F – P, on top of each other? That's the mark of an ancient brotherhood devoted to protecting binkle energy."

Jeep nods as the cryptic squiggle turns into something meaningful.

"Eight-foot pigmies? That's plain nonsense."

"That's not the way they look," laughs Adah. "It's just a symbol of something else."

Grikkl continues "Eight Foot Pygmies perform impossibly difficult tasks all over the world to interfere with Uuglash's demonic schemes. The work they do must be performed in total concealment because it's so dangerous.

Their duties put them at great risk. That's why no one can join the brotherhood until they've reached tablixx."

"Are you one?"

"Aye, Laddie, and proud it makes me. And Adah, too."

Adah smiles at Jeep, "What happened to you at Elkhorn proves you can reach tablixx." She looks expectantly at Grikkl, who adopts an official manner.

"Harump. Jeep, it gives me great pleasure to invite you into the Eight Foot Pygmies. The other members were informed of your feat and eagerly welcome you into their brotherhood."

Jeep is totally discombobulated, "Me?… Me? They're choosing me? I get to be an Eight Foot Pigmy?!"

Adah pats him on the back and smiles, "I always knew you could do something remarkable, Jeep I always knew…"

Grikkl explains further, "Before you stumbled on that blasted binkle-sucking machine, no one could figure out how Uuglash was getting enough energy for his cronies. His kind can't make high-octane energy like binkles, so they take it from others by force.

"We couldn't tell what he was doing to get so much of it. But we knew it was something we hadn't encountered before. His team kept getting stronger, somehow. You solved it, Jeep! You found out where their high-vibration energy supply was coming from.

"And you showed us how to stop them from doing it any more. By disturbing their power supply line their diabolical progress has been blocked—for a while anyway."

Jeep is flabbergasted, speechless, actually. Adah kept on patting his shoulder and beaming her great pride in him.

"There's one other little thing, Laddie… As you know, one of my responsibilities is maintaining the historical archives for the Chamber of Ancient Wisdom. That includes recording the noteworthy deeds and remarkable tales of the treasures. Your deed is worthy of being included here for all time."

"Me? Here? With all these heroes?" Jeep's remaining self-control dissolves.

Grikkl holds out his hand. "I want your compass, that catawampus compass you carry. It should be here, along with the enchanted mirror Adah gave you. They'll represent your extraordinary contribution."

Jeep opens his mouth but still no words come out. To say he is pleased would be far short of the truth—thrilled, tickled, amazed, and overjoyed would be more like it.

And Adah hands him another one, just as nice, saying, "We don't ever want you to get lost—especially now."

"Yup, I need my compass."

Adah adds, "Just so you know, Jeep, what you started isn't nearly finished yet. There'll be causes for celebration in the months and years ahead. You found out how and where

Uuglash gets his energy. When you wrecked his machine, you saved the patients at Elkhorn. And many more besides."

Grikkl adds, "Sure Adah, that's great, but there's another picture Jeep needs to think about. Elkhorn's one little place—think about the whole world. There are other places like Elkhorn with power-sucking machines harvesting energy for Uuglash's evil purposes. We need to shut them all down, wherever they do their vile work.

"That's where the Eight Foot Pygmies come in. That's the kind of assignment the members carry out. Thanks to you, we now know what to look for—a crazy spinning compass gives away the location of such machines.

"The Eight Foot Pigmies will destroy those diabolical binkle suckers as fast as we can find them."

Adah adds, "What a fine thing you've done! You should be proud."

"Plenty to be proud about, but let's not get sappy, Adah. Jeep is an Eight Foot Pigmy now. That means his part isn't done."

Grikkl looks Jeep straight in the eye, almost like they are equals. "Right Laddie? Can't you see that you need to be out there where the action is?"

"I'll try, but I don't know…"

"I'm sure that's good enough," says Adah. And nobody bothers to disagree.

Jeep grabs both of the genial gnomes and hugs them close. "You guys—this is such a binkle! I can recall my life before you found me—all cold, and lonely, and broken inside. That was bad enough. But much worse than that—binkle-less.

"You guys led me out of a scared life to where I know what's real, what's good just by its energy. I know I can't repay you, but I might do you a good turn in return."

"You don't owe us anything, Laddie."

"I know, but this is something the binkle taught me—that might could help you. Listen, anyway."

"Never one to think I know it all, have at it," says Grikkl.

"You know how you fall apart in the everyday world—that kittens hendrini thing? That spell uses magic to put Humpty Dumpty back together.

[An egg-shaped character in a nursery rhyme who falls off a wall and cannot be put back together again (late 17th century)]

"But wouldn't it be better if you didn't fall apart in the first place?"

"Sure, but I don't have any magic for that."

"That's not exactly true. It's not a magic spell that's needed—if I've got this figured out right. Down here and where you live there's binkle energy all over—so you don't have the cracking problem. Jeep looks from one gnome to the other to see if they are following.

Falling apart is caused by insufficient binkles, right?"

247

"Right. So…"

"Then just binkle yourself. And you'll have plenty of energy to hold yourself together to start with."

"What do you mean?"

Jeep explains, "Feel a binkle of gratitude *that you are not apart*—but all in one piece. That's the very energy that will hold you together. As long as you can feel the zizz from being together, you won't fall apart, or need a kittens hindrini spell to put you back together again."

"I think you're on to something there, Laddie. I never would have thought of it. I'll test that out."

"See Grikkl, the young ones can teach us all a thing or two," says Adah. "There's a binkle there for sure."

The next time Jeep visits her, Adah announces, "Let's have a tea party, right here—today! I've been wanting one—it's the perfect time." Her eyes sparkle, "Oh, Jeep, we'll have such fun!

Now, who should we invite?" She dances with excitement, like a kid headed to the circus.

"I know—I want to meet your mother, Helen… Definitely your mother. So, we'd better include her husband, too. Chris? Right? Oh, and we must have Anna and Louise, and MeToo, too. Cerberus can deliver invitations."

She quickly scribbles out several notes that include instructions about how to come: "At 3:00 this afternoon hold both your earlobes and say out loud, 'Adah sent for me' three times."

She places the notes in his pack and Cerberus leaps to his task.

Grikkl calls out, "Count me in."

"Well, there's one already. It's going to be perfect!"

Adah winks at Jeep. "Can't you feel it? We better get ready—there are a hundred things to do. We're going to make this place look festive." She rattles off a slew of tasks.

"Slow down. I'd better make a list."

Adah get Nelda involved and Grikkl clears his papers off the table.

"Enough for today. Adah, you seem to know what needs doing, but let me get it all done pronto."

Adah laughs. Jeep understands why as soon as Grikkl starts to play Arla, his concertina. The tune is lively to start with. But the faster he plays the faster everybody moves. Jeep's nimble feet never slow down as he swiftly whirls from task to task. The music exerts the same effect on the entire work crew.

Nelda and Jeep cover the table with a tablecloth that Adah had embroidered with colorful leaves and birds. Like her dress, the 3-D images are so realistic the cavern feels like they're outdoors—with living birds and plants.

More chairs appear at the table which grows bigger in order to seat a crowd. They cover the table with plates, glasses, and yummy-looking pastries and candies. Of course, it's an illusion since much of it is gussied-up faduki.

Bottles of Chadwick Soda cool in a tub of ice water. It has a dubahfruit and lime flavor that tickles the tongue—and the toes. Just the thing for a dance. But its most notable effect is as a laughter tonic. "More Laughs—More Often" is Chadwick Soda's slogan.

By the time Grikkl stops playing, Adah, Nelda, and Jeep are winded and giggly (that is, if Nelda could do either). It looks like a garden party, right and proper, they all agree.

First to arrive, Louise and Anna pop out of the air and bounce onto the sofa. Their faces are flushed with excitement. Adah hugs them and gives them a tour—which doesn't take long.

"Looks just like you described it—only better," Anna whispers to Jeep.

Chris and Helen arrive bearing two baskets. One holds MeToo. Chris holds out the other one to the hostess.

"I didn't come empty handed. Here are goodies made from truffles—truffle trifle and truffle crepes."

"I'm impressed! You actually cooked from scratch." Adah coos, (and so is everyone else who tastes them later). Adah hugs each of them in turn.

"You don't mind if I call you Helen and Chris, do you? No need for formality today."

Once Helen takes her seat, Heather and Yawn re-attach themselves beside her on the arms of the chair. And they don't move again. Helen sits quietly through the goings-on.

Everyone else squeezes around the table packed with fancy faduki goodies and Chris's truffle treats.

The food tastes great, but it can't compete with the company. Or the occasion of them all being together.

Almost immediately, a stifled giggle announces the arrival of unexpected guests.

"We heard there was a party going on," says a less wrinkly gnome who shimmers like Adah and Grikkl do. The twinkle in her laughing eyes leaves no doubt she squeezes all the delight possible out of every moment.

Her pudgy figure is decked out in a floor-length, lacy blue cape that seems to be festooned in rainbows. She strikes a grand pose, with her long gray hair streaming down her back.

Her companion is as thin as she is wide. His child's face, with super-big eyes, perches on a body tall enough to be a grown-up. But there isn't anything remotely grown-up about him or his manner.

He moves with such fluid grace he seems to flow—rather than walking in the usual way. From head to toe, he is covered in a forest green suit that clings to him as tightly as paint would.

Adah laughs and rolls her eyes. "All right you two—you're invited then. But you'll have to sing for your supper."

She turns toward those at the table, "Meet Layda and Taloo. You'd think they'd have seen enough of me the last few months. But noooooo, they still want to know what I'm up to. They can't stand to miss a party."

The new arrivals squeeze into the cozy circle. Taloo tells hilarious stories about the mischief of fairy folk, like how a dancing troupe caught a ride on a fox, but then didn't know how to slow it down so they could get off. Such a character! Everyone except Helen laughs until their sides ache.

Taloo shows off his newest trick. He rests his right hand on the floor, then stretches his left arm up until it actually touches the rock ceiling. Once both arms were solidly placed, he maneuvers his body around until both legs are stretched out straight, parallel to the floor.

Then he started to wiggle all over so fast he appears to be nothing but a blur. The rapid vibration creates a tone that echoes through the room and makes everyone tingle head to toe—further exaggerated by the Chadwick Soda.

"How can you do that, Taloo? Jeep wants to know.

"It's easier if you don't weigh much. Want to see me tie myself in a knot?" Taloo asks, as he twists his legs around each other and performs other absurd contortions.

Louise advises Jeep, "We don't want to see you trying to do that yourself."

"I think I can resist." Everyone bursts out laughing.

Adah and Layda sing several songs together. After The Bird Song, Louise whispers to Jeep, "The freedom of flying is even better than you described."

After that, Layda sings a song by herself, about water. It starts as a drop that falls from the clouds, hits the ground, and is sucked up through narrow roots. Then it moves through stems and leaves, before returning to the air, only to become a cloud again.

And sometimes, the water is only a drop, but at other times it is a puddle, or a river, or an ocean. And sometimes it is still, and at other times it is a waterfall or a torrent, driven by the wind. By the time Layda finishes, everyone there knew the ways of water.

As the song fades, a commotion arises—with noisy growls and vigorous banging. The ruckus came from MeToo and Nelda, as the dog rolls around on the ground. He growls and makes happy sounds as Nelda scratches and pets him all over. What an amusing pair—barking, humming, and bumping about.

Watching his dog having so much fun with Nelda makes Jeep think, *I wish it were me, too.*

Adah faces Louise and Anna. "My dears, Jeep told me about all your assistance in rescuing Helen. Even though plans changed at the last minute, your help made a big difference in its success."

She becomes serious, like a noble queen with an important task to do. "Suitable thanks must be given today. Louise, in honor of your worthy endeavors against the forces of darkness, I hereby present you a comb from Fairyland."

With great formality, she hands Louise a gold comb decorated with sparkly blue stones. In the manner she'd seen in movies, Louise curtsies deeply and says a soundless thank you. That response got her an approving royal nod from Adah.

Adah repeats the words to Anna and bestows another gold comb, only this one has green stones. Anna also curtsies deeply in grateful homage. The sisters feel like they'd been knighted.

Adah continues, "As you'll discover soon enough, my dears, these are enchanted combs. You'll never again have a bad hair day. Your hair must obey the comb's arrangement. It's is a small gift, really, but will remind you of the worthy role you both played in the never-ending war between good and evil."

The other guests applaud in tribute.

"Enough of such folderol," says Grikkl. "Let's have more treats and music."

He is persuaded to play Arla and tell the tale of how she came to him. So, the party continues on in the same light-hearted way.

All too soon, Taloo and Layda announce they have to go. After hugs all around, Layda says, "Let's all get together again some time," in the way that grown-ups do. In a twinkle they're both gone, leaving everyone breathless.

During the party, Helen's face held the same far-away look. She eats and listens, but without sharing in the fun.

Adah leans over and gently strokes Helen's cheek. "How sad for you. To know the value of love and caring, but to be unable to share them."

Chris puts his arm protectively around his wife. "It's hard to see her miss out on the love from Jeep and me. Glad as I am that she's healthier, she's still so empty."

Adah agrees. "I share your concern, Chris. "She focuses her full attention on Helen.

"My dear, Grikkl did a terrific job with you, to be sure. No one could have done more for you in all the world…" She pauses, letting the silence hang far too long.

"Except me." Adah sat without moving, waiting for her words to sink in.

"This is what I know. This is what I do. You all knew I've been in the land of babies before they're born. It's my job to fill their little krindles with binkles. Once in a while, a baby's krindle breaks, and I must fix it. It's not easily done, but I know how."

Adah holds Helen's hand in both of hers and stares into her eyes, "Helen, I want to do this for you, if you'll let me. I want to repair your krindle."

Helen doesn't answer, but everyone else around the table does. "Yes! Oh, yes! Do it!" they all exclaim as one.

And so, it came to be. Helen didn't recover overnight, even with Adah's exceptional skill. Yet Jeep detected fleeting signs of her old self almost from the beginning.

Helen was impatient to make up the lost time. She sang to herself—mostly sing-songing tunes from her childhood. Once again, she devised weird and silly ways to do everyday chores to keep the habit gods from taking over her mind. She and Chris hold hands and grin a lot. They'd go off by themselves, and on long ferry rides.

But what makes Jeep happiest is her delight in being near him. They talk and talk, just like before. Mother and son have healing to do. So, sharing memories about their time apart helps them rebuild their fragile, broken feelings.

The same kinds of discussions are happening between Helen and Chris, too. Each day, Helen can remember a few more details of her previous life.

She tells Jeep, "For the longest time, my brainpower was turned down so low it didn't work at all. I was about as smart as a turnip. But since my thoughts didn't hang together I didn't miss anything, didn't want anything. Nothing mattered much.

"The empty sameness changed for me after you began coming. One day, I felt you touch my arm—and I liked that. When you spoke to me the words didn't make sense, but I liked the sound of your voice.

"Once in a while, I knew who you were—but just for a moment. Oh Jeep, imagine how wonderful it is to go from being like that to how I am now. My life was given back to me."

"It was given back to both of us," Jeep corrects her.

"And Chris, too," she adds.

THE END

Turn the page for a note from Grikkl

A Note from Grikkl

Unlike books about fantastic adventures you can only imagine…
THE POWER OF THE BINKLE IS NOT MAKE BELIEVE.

It's REAL. It's ALIVE. (Oooh… I just felt a binkle just saying
that.) **The power of the binkle is within you**. It's a force
that can be drawn upon and directed to achieve great and
wonderful things. It connects you with everything you
admire—or aspire to become.

YOU ARE THE HERO AND THE STAR OF YOUR LIFE
ADVENTURE. And when you tap into Binkle Power, day in
and day out… your life changes. You become stronger. You get
along better with other people and yourself (I might add). The
forces of Nature open to you in ways you never even dreamed
of.

Reading this book is only the beginning. You have unleashed
Binkle Power in your life. Now here's a secret…

The more Binkles that you give to others… the more you have
for yourself.

Now that's Magic!

Grikkl

A Note from the Author, Faith Lynella

To: You and Fellow Binklers

Binkles are a powerful way to connect people, ideas, and noble visions. One way to keep them coming and strong within yourself is to spend time with other people you can binkle with (binklers).

Be always on the lookout for finding more of that energy. And keep it going. You have the advantage of knowing how vital it is in your life. Everything said about binkles in this book can work in real life. Let it be a force that helps protect you from negativity or from a heavy heart.

And one of the best way to get binkles is by sharing them and telling people how they work. So now, you have a mission that is in service to binkle power, and all the good that can come from it.

That will lead you into some wonderful life experiences for real. I wish you well in that. And ample binkles along the way.

The Binkle Mindset

There's much more to binkles than a few books. *It's a way of looking at what happens to you*. It is a way of finding healthy and upbeat energy in places it can easily be overlooked. It's a way of spotting what's important (and what isn't).

So, you gain more enjoyment in life. And it provides a measure of protection because you can recognize and avoid what could be harmful—no binkles. It's your own powerful energy source. And we all benefit from more of them in the world.

Since you know about binkles, they are part of you. And they will become more so as they open your eyes and open your heart to the energies of life. Please binkle any time you get the chance, and I can promise that you'll love what happens to you. Even better, tell your friends about them—you are already binkling with them, you know.

Binkles and joy to you,

Faith Lynella

Just because you finished this book, it doesn't mean you're done with what the book is about.

Jeep's Next Adventure

The next book in this series is

The Binkle and the Eight Foot Pigmies.

I hope You'll watch for it.

Made in United States
North Haven, CT
22 November 2023

44414639R00157